THE GHOSTS OF MERCY MANOR

BETTY REN WRIGHT

AN
APPLE
PAPERBACK

SCHOLASTIC INC.
New York Toronto London Auckland Sydney

for
Wyoma Cheney Baley

No part of this publication may be reproduced in whole or in part, or stored in a retrieval system, or transmitted in any form or by any means, electronic, mechanical, photocopying, recording, or otherwise, without written permission of the publisher. For information regarding permission, write to Scholastic Inc., 555 Broadway, New York, NY 10012.

ISBN 0-590-43602-3

12 11 10 9 8 7 6 5 4 3 2 1   9   4 5 6 7 8 9/9

Printed in the U.S.A.   40

112369

Chapter One

"Poor child," Mrs. Johnson moaned. "Whatever will happen to you now?"

Gwen Maxwell wobbled a little on her one-inch heels. She was twelve years old, but her friends at school said she looked thirteen, at least. I'm not a poor child, I'm practically grown-up, was what she wanted to say, but of course she couldn't. Not here. Not now.

"I haven't decided where I'll live," she said carefully. "My brother — "

"Oh, him." Mrs. Johnson looked across the lawn at Greg Maxwell with a disapproving air. "He's been a stranger here in Winfield for the last few years, hasn't he? And now it's too late for dear Mary to enjoy his visit."

Gwen searched for a means of escape. She

didn't want to talk to Mrs. Johnson about her future, and she didn't want to talk about Greg. She didn't even want to talk about Aunt Mary. She just wanted this long, sad day to be over.

"I'd better help to pass things," she said and ducked away to the lunch table set out in front of Aunt Mary's prized lilac bushes. Serving the little open-faced sandwiches would give her an excuse to move around the yard. If she was lucky, and quick, she wouldn't have to hear that terrible question one more time.

Whatever will happen to you now?

The question was terrible because Gwen didn't know the answer. Her mother and father had died five years ago in a car accident, and she still remembered the loneliness of the days that followed. She didn't belong anywhere; there was no one left to love, or to love her, except a big brother she hardly knew. Then Great-Aunt Mary had appeared, like a fairy godmother in a nursery tale, and had brought her to live in this spotless little house on Barker Drive.

If she'd found it difficult to welcome a little girl into her life, Aunt Mary had never said so. She'd set up a twin bed in her sewing room and had taken seven-year-old Gwen to Forest Park School to enroll in the second grade. Aunt Mary had come to all the school programs, had admired Gwen's drawings, and had given her a quarter each time she got an A on a test. Even though she was seventy years older than Gwen, she'd tried hard to do all the things the other children's mothers did.

"I wish you had a great big family," she'd said once. "But we make the best of it, don't we?" And they had.

At the funeral this afternoon Gwen realized that in those five years she had never said "I love you" to her great-aunt, and Aunt Mary had never said those words to her. But they had loved each other. Now the loneliness, the feeling of being lost, had returned, and this time there was no fairy godmother to come to her rescue. No one but Greg.

"Would you like a sandwich?"

The circle of church ladies gathered around her brother shook their heads, and Greg went on talking. Mrs. Johnson had been right; he was a stranger. Fifteen years older than Gwen, he was more like an uncle than a brother.

She offered the sandwich plate to Liz, Greg's young, blonde bride, knowing she would refuse. "Snacking is bad for your complexion," she'd told Gwen the day they arrived from Phoenix. She'd looked with disapproval at the piece of chocolate cake Gwen was eating. "You'll get horrible spots if you eat that junk."

The chocolate cake had been one of Aunt Mary's specialties, a treat she had always made for church bake sales and for Gwen's birthday. Liz didn't know that, Gwen had reminded herself quickly, but the words had stung.

She went back to the table and picked up a plate of cookies, then put it down. People were starting to leave. The bright little garden would soon return to its quiet self. Gwen said good-bye to the minister and to four ladies from the League of Women Voters. Then she wandered into the house and stood in front of the bathroom mirror for a while, brushing her shoulder-length brown hair. Brushing helped her think. She had to have a plan, something she could do to fight panic.

She decided that as soon as all the guests had gone, she would tell Greg how much she was looking forward to living with them in Phoenix. Don't ask them, tell them — isn't that what Aunt Mary would have advised? They had to take her with them. They had to! She had nowhere else to go.

When she went back outside, Liz was walking toward the front of the house with the last of the visitors but one. Greg was talking to a woman Gwen hadn't noticed before. She was a small, tired-looking person who kept looking around while they talked. When she saw Gwen, her brown eyes warmed and she smiled shyly. Gwen smiled back but stayed where she was, close to the kitchen door. She wanted the woman to leave. It would be easier to confront Greg if she could do it before Liz returned to the backyard.

"Gwen, come on over here."

Reluctantly, Gwen started across the yard toward her brother, kicking off her shoes as she walked. For no good reason, she was frightened. Perhaps it was Greg's strained expression. Or maybe it was because the woman's smile now seemed frozen in place. When Gwen reached them she saw tears shining in the woman's big, dark eyes.

"This is Gwen, Mrs. Mercy. Gwen, this is Mrs. Mercy. You two are going to like each other a lot. I can tell it already."

Gwen stared at him. What was he talking about? Why were she and this — this Mercy person going to like each other? What difference did it make whether they liked each other or not?

The woman put out a hand and touched Gwen's wrist. "We've been talking about your loss," she said in a sweet, husky voice. "This must be very hard for you. You miss your aunt terribly, I'm sure."

"Yes, I do." What was going on here?

Greg cleared his throat and ran a hand over his hair. "Of course she misses Aunt Mary," he said heartily. "But at least she isn't going to have to leave all her friends here in Wisconsin, thanks to you, Mrs. Mercy. That's good news, isn't it, Gwen?"

Gwen looked at him uncertainly. Mrs. Mercy's eyes grew darker, as though she understood Gwen's confusion and regretted it.

"Your brother means you're going to come to live with us, Gwen," she explained. "I know we can't take your aunt's place, but we'll do our best to make you happy." She faltered as Gwen stared at her, unable to speak. "Our boy Jason is growing up fast, and our little girl Tessie would love a big sister, and we have lots of room now, so we — we just decided to offer ourselves as foster-parents. And the Social Services people told us about you and — and it, well, just sounded perfect — "

"No!" Gwen found her voice at last. "That isn't right! I'm going to go to — " She looked into Greg's flushed face and left the sentence unfinished. She wasn't going to Phoenix. All the time she'd been making her plans, her brother had been looking for another answer. He was going to make her live with strangers.

"You know I'd really like to have you with us, Gwen," Greg said hurriedly. "But it's impossible right now. Liz and I were married just six months ago," he told Mrs. Mercy when Gwen refused to meet his eyes. "My wife is working and furnishing our apartment and . . . well, it isn't the answer, I'm afraid."

So that was it. Liz refused to have her. Out of the corner of her eye, Gwen saw her sister-in-law come around the side of the house and stop short.

"I'm sure Gwen understands," Mrs. Mercy said. She and Greg were both watching her anxiously. They were partners, allied against her, willing her to be a good girl and go along with what had already been decided.

Gwen felt as if she might choke on the hard lump of hurt that had settled in her throat. Nobody wanted Gwen Maxwell for herself. Foster-parents were paid to take care of people no one else wanted.

Might as well go along with what you can't change — that probably would have been Aunt Mary's comment. You'll save yourself a lot of grief. Gwen glanced at the curtain of lilacs and leaves in front of her and thought she'd give anything in the world if she could look up and see Aunt Mary coming across the lawn. She took a deep breath and filled her lungs with the fragrance that would always mean home and safety.

"It's okay," she said finally and heard Greg's sigh of relief.

But it wasn't okay. She was remembering how it had felt to be seven years old and not belong anywhere. Nothing had changed. Once again she was alone, and she hated it.

Chapter Two

"I think it's just awful!" Julie McElroy scooped some sweaters from a dresser drawer and dropped them into a carton. "But at least you don't have to move away. And we'll go to middle school together this fall, just the way we planned."

Gwen rolled up a pair of jeans and handed them to her best friend to drop on top of the sweaters. "You sound like my brother," she said. "That's all he talked about at supper last night — how lucky I was to be staying here in Winfield. And Liz kept saying yes-yes-yes, as if they were only letting me stay with those Mercys because it was what *I* wanted."

"But you do want to stay here, don't you?" Julie looked hurt. "I'm glad you're staying."

"That's not the point. Greg is my family — we should stick together now." Gwen threw herself on the bed and stared up at the ceiling. She couldn't tell even Julie how she felt about being sent to live with strangers. "I think Greg wants to invite me," she said glumly, "but Liz won't let him. She's coming between us." She nodded to herself, liking the way that sounded.

"You're probably right," Julie agreed. "But what can you do about it?"

"I'll think of something."

"Besides, you said Mrs. Mercy seemed kind of nice." Julie watched her anxiously.

Gwen shrugged. "They live way out on Blue Mill Road. I'll never be able to come to town unless someone brings me. I probably won't see you all summer."

"We'll talk on the phone," Julie promised. "And I'll call you as soon as we get back from our vacation."

Gwen had forgotten about the McElroys' annual trip to Oregon. Without wanting to, she pictured Julie and her little brothers and her parents riding along the highway, eating ice-cream bars and singing. A family vacation must be fun. "How long will you be gone?" she asked wistfully.

"Three weeks. My grandma and grandpa have

all kinds of stuff planned for us to do."

Three weeks. Gwen fought back another wave of panic. Three weeks sounded like forever.

"Oregon sounds neat," she said, trying to act unconcerned. "You can tell me all about it when you get back, and I'll tell you what's happened to me."

Julie brightened. "You'll be having a good time, too," she said. "It'll be exciting, living in a new place — an adventure, right?" They stared at each other uneasily, trying to believe that was true.

Mrs. Mercy arrived at ten the next morning, looking more cheerful than she had at the funeral. Gwen watched from her bedroom window as Greg carried her suitcase and boxes out to the driveway and stowed them in the back of the station wagon next to several bags of groceries. He and Mrs. Mercy talked, with frequent glances toward the door.

When Gwen finally came out, they both looked relieved.

"Did you say good-bye to Liz?" Greg asked.

Gwen nodded. "She's packing. She said you're going home this afternoon."

"Right," Greg said. "Can't stay away from the office too long. But I'll be back this fall to check

11

with Aunt Mary's attorney on the sale of the house and so on. You and I'll have a good long visit then." He bent and gave her a quick kiss on the cheek. "You write and tell me all about yourself. I'll be waiting to hear."

"Okay." Gwen slid into the passenger seat and fastened her seatbelt. "Will you write back?"

"Of course I will." He sounded shocked that she could doubt it.

"And can I come to Phoenix later on?"

He stepped back from the car. "We'll talk about it."

Gwen wanted to ask whether he meant he and she would talk about it or he and Liz would talk. But before she could shape the question, Mrs. Mercy broke in. "I'm afraid we have to be on our way," she said, switching on the ignition. "I promised the sitter I'd be back by ten to pick up Tessie. Tessie's my little girl," she explained as she backed the car out of the drive. "She can hardly wait to meet you, Gwen."

Greg stood in the driveway watching them go, an unhappy expression on his face.

"He's wondering if he's doing the right thing, poor man." Mrs. Mercy turned the wheel sharply and started down Barker Drive. "I know the feeling well. When you grow up, you wonder about that a lot."

"Grown-ups can do anything they want to do," Gwen said. She knew she sounded sulky, but she didn't care. "Grown-ups are lucky."

Mrs. Mercy gave a little chuckle. "It's not that simple, Gwen," she said. "You'll find out for yourself some day."

They drove in silence until they reached Hayes Avenue. Then Gwen sat up straight and pointed down the block. "That's my school. I mean, it was my school. I start middle school in September — unless I'm in Phoenix by then. I don't know if they have middle schools in Phoenix."

Mrs. Mercy hesitated for only a second, then changed the subject. "And here's where our baby-sitter lives. Tessie usually stays with her while I do my errands in town. Three and a half is a wonderful age — but *not* in a supermarket."

The station wagon rolled to a stop, and Gwen waited while Mrs. Mercy went into the little gray house. When she returned, she was hand-in-hand with a tiny copy of herself. Tessie's hair was shaped in the same smooth, dark cap, and her huge brown eyes regarded Gwen solemnly as Mrs. Mercy introduced them.

"This is Gwen, honey."

"Hi, Tessie."

The shy smile was like Mrs. Mercy's, too. I've always wanted a little sister. The thought startled

Gwen, and she was glad she hadn't said it out loud. That would be just what Mrs. Mercy — and, of course, Greg — would like to hear.

Tessie let herself be strapped into the seat in back and sat quietly while her mother drove and told Gwen about the rest of the family.

"My husband — Frank — works at First State Bank here in Winfield. We bought our farm from my aunt and uncle's estate a couple of years ago. Frank doesn't farm it himself — we rent the land to other people. The other member of the family is Jason, our son. He's sixteen. It'll be nice to have someone fairly close to your own age around, won't it?" She looked at Gwen as if she wasn't sure of the answer. "I want you to call me Dena," she continued. "Mrs. Mercy is so formal. It'll take a while for you to feel at home, I suppose, but just give it time, Gwen. Do you think you'll like country living?"

"I don't know," Gwen said. "I've never tried it before." She felt Tessie's dark brown gaze and realized she sounded cold. "I guess it could be fun," she added without conviction. "Nature and all that."

"No cows," Tessie spoke for the first time, sounding mournful.

Her mother laughed. "Tessie thinks a farm without cows doesn't deserve the name," she said.

"Her favorite picture book says a farm is supposed to have them."

"My Aunt Mary grew up on a farm," Gwen said over her shoulder. "Her father gave her a calf when she was just a little older than you are, and she raised it. It won a blue ribbon at the county fair."

Silence greeted this information, and Gwen was immediately sorry she had offered it. There was no reason to make conversation with the Mercys. They might think she was glad to be riding along with them through the countryside, and if they thought that, they would be very wrong. She was there because she had no choice.

They had left the Winfield town limits behind, and now they turned off the highway. Houses dropped away, and rolling fields took their place. Two more turns and they were on a gravel road, crunching along between fields of young corn. The road sloped gently and curved again.

"There it is," Dena said abruptly, as they plunged through a scattering of trees and out into the open once more. "Welcome to Mercy Manor, Gwen. That's what my husband calls it when he wants to sound grand."

"Our house," said the little voice from the back seat. "It's big."

It certainly was big — and beautiful. Gwen felt

her heart lift with unexpected pleasure. In spite of its size, the old farmhouse had a cozy, inviting look. The white clapboard was freshly painted, and a long porch curved around two sides like an enfolding arm. You could sit out on that porch at night and look at the stars and listen to country noises and watch cars go by, Gwen thought. No, she corrected herself, no cars. Mercy Manor stood at the very end of Blue Mill Road. No one would drive by because there was no place to go.

They turned into the yard and parked next to a barn.

"Frank's at work, but Jason should be around someplace," Dena Mercy said. "We'll leave your things in the car, and most of the groceries, and he'll carry them in for us. I'll just take the meat in now. . . . Your room is up there on the left." She pointed to a back window on the second floor, then turned to open the gate of the station wagon. "Tessie's room is across the hall from it."

Gwen looked up and was startled to meet another pair of eyes. A thin face framed by long blonde hair stared down from what must be Tessie's bedroom window.

"Who's that?" Dena hadn't mentioned another girl in the family.

Mrs. Mercy straightened with a grocery bag in her arms, her expression suddenly wary.

"Who's who?" she asked. There was an edge to her voice that Gwen hadn't heard before.

Gwen started to point and then stopped in confusion. The window was empty. "I thought I saw a girl up there," she said. "She was looking down at us. . . ."

"Not a chance," Dena Mercy said with that same unexpected sharpness. "There's no one here but us chickens. Except for Jason, of course, and no doubt he's busy with one of his projects." She started across the yard to the back porch. "Come on, ladies. We're home."

Your home, not mine, Gwen corrected her silently. Uneasy and a little frightened, she kept her eyes on the empty window as she followed Dena to the house. Was it possible that she had imagined the girl?

She might have convinced herself of that if she hadn't turned just then to see if Tessie was coming. The little girl was standing next to the car, looking up at her bedroom window with a wondering expression, as if she had seen someone there, too.

Chapter Three

"Let's take Gwen on a tour of the house, Tessie."
Dena Mercy put the packages of meat in a refrigerator that was covered with pictures of
sunrises, old-fashioned gardens, and smiling children. "She's seen the kitchen — let's show her
the dining room and the living room. We don't
want her to get lost, do we?"

Tessie giggled. She had abandoned her shyness
at the back door, and now she clutched Gwen's
hand and pulled her across the kitchen into the
spacious dining room.

"This is where I sit, and this is where you'll
sit, Gwennie," she danced around the table.
"Right next to me." She darted through the wide
double doors at one side of the room, and Gwen
and Dena followed.

"This foyer is supposed to be the main entrance," Dena commented, "but it doesn't get much use. The house was built with its back to the road for some strange reason, and we like it that way. You can sit on the front porch or the side one and see nothing but grass and fields and woods."

A graceful flight of stairs led up from the hall, and beyond them, on the other side of the foyer, were more double doors leading into the longest living room Gwen had ever seen.

"One of these days we must do some serious furniture shopping," Dena said apologetically. "I'm used to seeing it this way, but when I show the rooms to someone else, I realize . . ." Her voice trailed off. "Most of the furniture is what came from our old house, and that was a lot smaller than this one."

"It's really nice," Gwen said. She liked the shining wood floors and the fresh, sweet breezes that blew in through every window. It was true that there wasn't much furniture, but the living room couch and chairs were upholstered in bright colors and there was a blue vase full of wildflowers on the low, round coffee table. A poster of mountains bathed in mist was taped next to the archway.

"We haven't gotten around to hanging pictures," Dena said. "Doing that seems so — I don't know — so final. Instead, the wall decorations come and go. When I see something I like, I put it up where we can all enjoy it for a while. You can put up some pictures if you want — there are lots of walls."

Gwen went over to the wide bay window and looked out at a meadow that stretched beyond the lawn. She wouldn't put up any pictures. That would be like saying this was her home, the place where she belonged.

They went back into the front hall and climbed the stairs, Tessie running noisily ahead. She stopped on the landing halfway up and twirled in the multicolored beams of light streaming through a fan-shaped stained-glass window.

"Look at me!" she squealed. "Look at me dance!"

"I used to do that when I was a little girl," Dena said. "This house belonged to my aunt and uncle then, and I stayed with them for a few weeks one summer while my folks were in Europe. I was only five, and the house was magic to me — for a while, anyway. So many corners to hide in, and the stained-glass panels and — oh, well." Her smile faded. "Good things come to an end, don't they?" she said wryly, as if she were thinking of the changes in Gwen's life as well as in her own.

The upstairs was divided by a long hallway. The Mercys' big bedroom was in the front of the house, and opposite it was a closed door with a KEEP OUT sign taped to the door.

"That says don't come in," Tessie explained. "It's Jason's room."

"And it's full of important treasures," Dena added. "None of which may be touched by his little sister."

"My room's nicer, anyway," Tessie announced. "It's the best." She led the way down the hall, past closets and a bathroom to the rear of the house, then danced through a door on the left. Gwen followed her.

"Do you like it?" Tessie demanded. "Is it nice?"

"It's great," Gwen said enthusiastically. "Like a room in a picture book." She admired the oval rag rug, the narrow bed complete with ruffled canopy, the child-sized rocking chair and table, the toy shelves, the bright pictures on the wall. It really was perfect.

"This is the only room I've gotten around to furnishing properly," Dena said from the doorway. "I wanted it to be a happy place." Her voice faded off, and for a moment the sad look Gwen had noticed the day before was back. Then the tour continued. "The door next to this one leads up to the attic," Dena explained. "And your room is right across the hall. It's the one I had when I was a child. These stairs take you down to the back hall and the kitchen."

Gwen followed Dena out of Tessie's room reluctantly. The little bedroom, furnished with such love and care, was a comforting place. Leaving it, Gwen felt more lonely than ever.

A screen door slammed below them, and footsteps thudded up the back stairs, two steps at a time. A tall, thin boy catapulted into the hall and stopped short when he saw Gwen.

"This noise machine is our son Jason," Dena said fondly, as she put an arm around the newcomer. "Jason, this is Gwen. I hope you'll mind your manners and help to make her welcome."

"Hi." He sounded breathless. His brown eyes watched Gwen warily, and one hand came up to cover the scattering of pimples on his chin. "Nice — nice to meet you." He looked pleadingly at his mother. "I have some stuff to put away in my room, okay?"

"Okay." Dena released him. "But then go down to the car and bring in the rest of the groceries, please. And Gwen's suitcase and her cartons. Bring her things up here right away. We want her to get settled in as quickly as possible."

Jason ducked his head and rushed down the hall to his room, shutting the door firmly behind him.

"He's shy," his mother murmured. "Give him time." She motioned Gwen across the hall, and once again Tessie led the way.

The room that was to be Gwen's was small and sunny, with sheer white panels on the windows and a single bed against one wall. An old-fashioned bureau and a rocker, both painted white, stood opposite the bed, and there was a small bedside table and reading lamp. A patchwork quilt provided the only color in the room.

"You can fix it up any way you want to," Dena said. "Decide what you want on the walls, and we can pick out a rug together. Maybe you'd like a braided one like Tessie's?"

"That'd be nice," Gwen tried to sound enthusiastic. The bare, impersonal little room, so different from the one across the hall, chilled her, but she didn't want to hurt Dena's feelings. It doesn't matter, she reminded herself. I'm not going to stay long, anyway.

As they walked from room to room in Mercy Manor, Gwen's determination had been growing. No matter what Dena said, this was the Mercys' home, not Gwen's. She belonged with her own family, and if Greg didn't understand that, she would have to convince him and Liz. She couldn't be dropped into other people's lives like a stray puppy, to be looked after and pitied.

Later, when Jason had brought up her luggage and deposited it just outside the bedroom door, she kicked off her sneakers and lay on the patchwork quilt. Downstairs, she could hear Tessie telling her mother what kind of cookies to bake. I'll write to Greg and Liz every week, she planned. No, two or three times a week. I'll make them want me!

When she opened her eyes again, Tessie was peeking in at her. "Lunch," she announced importantly. "You were taking a nap."

Gwen sat up. "I'm wide-awake now," she said and looked around at the little room glowing with sunlight. Something was different, but she didn't know what. There were the white walls and curtains, the chest of drawers, the rocker, the bedside table with its lamp — and a rose.

Gwen picked up the flower. It was made of paper cleverly folded to form petals. A twist of green wire provided the stem.

"Is this something your mom saved because it's so pretty?" she asked curiously. "Like the poster in the living room?"

Tessie shook her head. "She leaves the rose in my room sometimes," she said softly. "And then she takes it away."

"Your mom does that?"

The little girl frowned. "The girl does it."

"What girl?"

But Tessie darted away. "Just nobody," she said. "My mom says it's nobody. And you're supposed to come to lunch," she called from halfway down the back stairs. "We're having chocolate milk."

Gwen laid the rose on the table. For a minute, in spite of the sunshine and birdsong, she was frightened; then she brushed the fear away. Tessie obviously wasn't supposed to talk about the girl, but there had to be a reasonable explanation. All she had to do was ask Dena.

Yet, as she went down the stairs to the kitchen, she knew she wouldn't ask. If she did, she might sound as if she were interested in what went on in the Mercys' house. She wasn't.

Still, the rose had given her a beginning for her first letter to Greg and Liz. You'd better send me a plane ticket right away, she would write. Something kind of weird is going on here.

Chapter Four

"Jason! Get out here! I thought I told you to cut the grass today!"

The furious bellow from the backyard warned Gwen that she was about to meet the fourth member of the Mercy family. She stepped back quickly from the kitchen sink, clutching the bouquet of wildflowers Tessie had brought her a few minutes earlier. One glance through the window at the big man climbing out of a car, his face red with anger, told her this wasn't the right moment for introductions.

Footsteps sounded overhead, moving slowly from the front to the back of the house. Dena Mercy went to the foot of the back stairs and looked up reproachfully.

"I didn't know you were supposed to cut the

grass," she said. "Why didn't you do it?"

The footsteps descended. "Didn't have time," Jason mumbled. "I had a lot of stuff to do."

"You and your stuff." Dena sighed and came into the kitchen. "You'll have to get used to this, I'm afraid, Gwen," she said, forcing a smile. "Jason and his father have different ideas about what's important."

Jason reached the bottom of the stairs and paused before going outside. "That's for sure," he muttered and let the screen door slam behind him.

For the next few minutes Gwen busied herself with the flowers and tried not to hear the angry voice in the backyard.

Dena watched her trim the stems to different lengths. "You're doing a good job, Gwen. You'll have to do all our flower-arranging from now on." Her voice shook a little, and she looked as if the sounds from the backyard disturbed her more than she wanted to admit.

" . . . RIGHT NOW!" The shouted order seemed to signal an end to the scolding. Gwen risked another peek from the window and saw Jason trudging across the yard. His father stood, arms folded across his chest, and waited till the roar of a tractor-mower sounded from inside the barn. Then he turned toward the house.

Dena darted across the room to the back hall and returned almost at once, pulling her husband by the hand. He looked startled and embarrassed when he saw Gwen standing there.

"I forgot. This was the day!" He smacked his forehead with a huge fist, then shook Gwen's hand energetically.

"Sorry you had to hear an explosion first thing. That kid — " For a moment his bad humor seemed about to return.

"Arguments don't bother me," Gwen said, though that wasn't quite true. Aunt Mary had never scolded; she had just spoken her mind in a soft voice and then remained quiet for a while.

"Anyway, it's nice to have you with us," Frank Mercy said heartily, and Gwen could tell he meant it. Like Dena, he had a warm smile. It reminded her a little of her father's smile in the picture that stood on her dresser upstairs.

Dinner that evening was uncomfortable, even though Dena tried hard to keep a conversation going. Frank Mercy and Jason ignored each other, and Gwen concentrated on her chicken and mashed potatoes, acutely aware of being an outsider in this family circle. Afterward, Jason went back outside to finish the mowing, and Gwen helped with the dishes. The familiar chore made her feel worse than ever; it should be Aunt

Mary standing at the sink, not this almost-stranger. Without warning, tears spilled down her cheeks as she thought about all that had happened in the last week.

"I'll be right back," she choked, and dashed up the back stairs to the privacy of her bedroom.

"Gwen!" Dena sounded alarmed. "What's wrong?"

"I'm all right," she called before closing the door. If she was going to cry, she wanted to be by herself.

It was several minutes before she noticed that the rose was gone. Tessie probably took it, she told herself. It must be all part of some game she plays. Not that it mattered. She buried her face in the pillow. Nothing mattered except the fact that she was alone.

Gwen found it hard to get to sleep that night. The trees rustled in the night wind, and a whole concert of insect sounds seemed to be telling her she was in someone else's house. The Mercys were nice people, but they weren't her family. All the family she had was in Phoenix.

The second night at Mercy Manor was no better, and the third night was worse. Gwen lay awake for hours, thinking of the house on Barker Drive where she'd gone to bed with nothing to worry about but the next test at school or what she would do over the weekend. This must be what it's like to be caught in an earthquake, she thought, recalling scenes from television news. One minute your life is great and you don't even think about how lucky you are, and the next minute everything's changed.

During the day Tessie was a lively companion, but their rambles through the meadow that stretched beyond the lawn failed to tire Gwen out. She offered to help around the house, but Dena usually told her to do whatever she wanted to do. "You can help, but you're not here to work all the time — you're part of our family," she said repeatedly, as if she had guessed Gwen's thoughts on that subject. "Have fun — just stay out of the woods, please. It's not a very big area, but Tessie could easily get lost if she wandered in by herself." Dena's expression turned grim at the thought. "There are plenty of other places to walk. And after school starts, you won't have much time for hiking."

School. Gwen stared up at the ceiling over her bed. She didn't want to think that far ahead. School and Julie seemed a million years off. There were other friends in Winfield she could call, of course, but she wasn't ready to talk to any of them. No one else knew she was living in a foster home because her brother's wife didn't want to be bothered with her. Every time she thought of people finding out, she felt like hiding her head under the covers.

A sharp crack outside her bedroom door made her catch her breath. It sounded as if Tessie's door had opened, but surely she wouldn't get out of bed in the dark without calling for someone. Unless — unless she walked in her sleep! Gwen had never known a sleepwalker, but she supposed it was something that could happen to very young children as well as to grown-ups. And there were steep stairs at either end of the hall!

She slipped out of bed, curling her toes against the bare floor. Cautiously, she eased the bedroom door open and peered out into the hall. Tessie's door loomed dark and tightly closed. For a moment there was no sound at all, and then the creaking began once more, so close that she almost cried out. Someone was on the back stairs.

Gwen leaned out into the bar of moonlight that streamed in through the small window above the staircase, in time to see the top of a head just descending out of sight. Long, smooth golden hair — it was the girl she had glimpsed in Tessie's window! It had to be. She was here, creeping through the house while the family slept.

But this was no ordinary prowler. In the second or two before the girl disappeared down the steps, Gwen realized that the stream of moonlight was unbroken; the pale glow shone right through the golden curtain of hair.

Gwen eased her door shut and darted back into bed, her heart thudding. She lay rigid, her eyes on the doorknob. If she heard the footsteps again, if the door opened, she was sure she would die of fright.

For what seemed like hours she waited. At last she drifted into a restless, dream-muddled sleep, awaking with relief to a room full of sunshine. It was eight o'clock; she could hear the clatter of dishes downstairs and Tessie's high voice.

"Good! You had a nice long sleep," Dena said brightly when Gwen joined them in the kitchen. "Frank left an hour ago, and Jason is biking into town to get something he says he absolutely needs. You just help yourself to cereal and toast, and I'll have another cup of coffee to keep you company. Good excuse."

"You and I are going to have a picnic today," Tessie announced. "Just us. At the river."

"If Gwen would like to," Dena said warningly. "I told you, Tessie, Gwen may have plans of her own."

"I just want to write a letter to my brother

first," Gwen said. "There are some things I have to talk to him about."

She had thought some more about her letter last night while she lay waiting for whatever might happen next. At first she had planned to mention the mystery of the "ghost-girl" only casually, but the figure on the stairs had changed that. What Gwen had seen was much too frightening to be treated lightly. . . . Greg, I'm so scared. I can't sleep in this house. . . . I don't know what to do. . . . Surely her brother and Liz would realize they had to come to her rescue.

Dena was watching her curiously. "A picnic sounds fine," Gwen said. "Maybe we can go swimming in the river."

Dena shook her head. "Wading, maybe," she said, "but that's all. Trout River is actually just a stream now — it's shrunk a good deal since they built a dam near town. But it's still a pleasant place to sit and have your lunch. . . . Gwen, is something wrong? Besides missing your great-aunt and your brother, I mean. You look so worried. Is there something I can do?"

Gwen took a deep breath. "It's just that I didn't sleep very well last night," she said carefully. "I thought — I thought I heard someone walking in the hall."

Dena set her coffee cup down with a sharp clink. "A dream, probably. Or somebody going to the bathroom. Or else it was just one of the noises this old house makes every so often — all houses have their own noises, you know. You'll get used to them."

Gwen kept her eyes on her cereal bowl. "But I thought I saw someone, too. Going down the stairs. It was a girl with long blonde hair."

"Well, that just proves it was a dream, doesn't it?" Dena said with a strained little laugh. "We don't have any long-haired blondes in this family."

"Mama, maybe — " Tessie had clearly been about to make a suggestion but changed her mind under her mother's gaze.

" — maybe we should concentrate on what kinds of sandwiches you ladies want to take on your picnic," Dena finished the sentence for her. "Egg salad or peanut butter, Tessie?"

"Peanut butter! And olives in a little cup. I'll get them." Tessie ran to the refrigerator.

And that was the end of the conversation about the girl with golden hair. Clearly, Tessie wasn't supposed to talk about her, and neither was Gwen. But how could they live together in one house and not admit to each other that something unexplainable was happening here?

The girl had been there in the hallway last night. She had gone down the back stairs, her hair gleaming in the moonlight. Dena could change the subject, but she couldn't change the facts.

Chapter Five

Jason was weeding a marigold bed when Gwen wandered outside after breakfast. They had hardly spoken since her arrival; he was busy with his own affairs all day, and at mealtimes he ate hurriedly and waited with obvious impatience for the others to finish. Tessie was the only one who seemed able to make him smile.

Gwen watched for a moment, then dropped to her knees and began weeding. "I used to do this with my Aunt Mary," she offered. "Only she had nasturtiums and pansies, mostly. She said they were nice-little-old-lady flowers."

To her surprise, Jason looked up with a grin. "That's good. Nice-little-old-lady flowers. These marigolds are different — they're tough. I don't know why I ever have to weed 'em. They can take care of themselves. Same with the irises and the daylilies on the other side of the house. You can't keep them down. My mom likes them because they're the flowers her aunt and uncle had growing here when she stayed with them when she was a little girl. She said living here made her feel like a princess," he added with amusement. "How about that?"

Gwen thought she understood. It would be easy to pretend this house was an isolated castle, guarded on one side by dense woods and on the others by meadows and fields.

"All it needs is a moat," she suggested. "And some knights and dragons, of course."

Jason leaned back on his heels and wiped his forehead. "The house is okay, I guess. There's a lot of yard work, though. And guess who gets to do it all? I'd rather spend my time on other things."

"Like what?" Gwen asked bluntly, but bluntness didn't work. The closed-off look returned to Jason's face, and he moved around her to work farther along the flower bed.

"Just stuff."

She weeded for a few more minutes in silence, then went back inside. Dena was polishing the dining room table, and Tessie was busy in the living room. Dena's expression was somber, and she rubbed the table energetically, as if she were trying to banish an unwanted thought.

"Is there something I can do?" Gwen asked. She wondered if Dena's mood was the result of their talk about the ghost-girl.

"Not a thing," Dena assured her. "Why don't you write your letter now?"

Gwen hesitated. "This is such a great house," she said softly. "I can see why you love it."

Dena looked up then. "Sometimes I love it, and sometimes I don't," she said bleakly. "Today is one of the days when I think we never should have moved. The place — well, it just depresses me, and I wish we'd stayed in town."

"Why does it depress you?" Gwen asked, hoping to hear more. But Dena just shrugged and returned to her polishing. The only sound was the buzzing of insects against the screens.

Later, curled up in the rocker in her bedroom, Gwen tried to put her feelings into words her brother would understand.

. . . The Mercys are really good people, but they have their own problems, and they don't need another one — ME! Besides, there's something strange going on here — don't laugh — I think this house is haunted. . . ." She paused, suddenly certain that hardheaded Greg *would* laugh. Her description of the

ghost-girl wouldn't move him at all. She could picture him showing her letter to Liz and shaking his head over his little sister's silliness.

Carefully she inked out the last sentence and started a new paragraph. *I don't belong here. I can't sleep at night, and I can't see my friends, and . . .* She stopped again. What if Greg called Dena Mercy to find out why she wouldn't allow Gwen to spend time in town with her friends from school? *But she hasn't even asked! Dena would say,* and that was true.

Discouraged, Gwen crumpled up the sheet of paper and dropped it in the wastebasket. It was as hard to confide in Greg in a letter as it had been in person. Yet somehow she had to make him see that she belonged with him. *I'm not an orphan!* she wanted to shout across the miles. *I have a family. This isn't fair!*

Tessie appeared at the door just then, her face bright with anticipation. "Mama says we can go on the picnic when you're ready," she announced. "Are you ready?"

"Sure." Gwen stretched her legs and stood up, glad of an excuse to postpone the letter-writing. They clattered down the stairs together, collected the box lunches waiting in the refrigerator, and in a few minutes were on their way.

The narrow path leading toward the river began in a corner of the front yard close to the woods.

"We can't go in there — not ever," Tessie reminded her. "Mama wouldn't like it. You can get lost in there."

Gwen shrugged. She'd rather be out in the sunshine where, she soon discovered, it was hard to go on feeling sorry for herself. Her spirits rose as she chatted with Tessie and helped the little girl over a battered wooden fence that edged the far end of the meadow. On the other side, long rows of unfamiliar plants marched ahead of them.

"These are sunflowers," Tessie explained importantly. "Pretty soon they'll be as tall as — as anything! And there'll be millions of sunflower seeds. I love 'em."

She led the way between the rows of plants to the far end of the field where a scattering of willows marked the bank of the Trout River.

"We'll have our picnic right here." She pointed to a nest of flat stones close to the water. "That's where Mama and I always sit."

"Fine." Gwen dropped down on one of the rocks and stretched out on the sun-warmed surface. For the moment, at least, she felt relaxed, even contented. Tessie lay beside her for about thirty seconds, then jumped up to gather handfuls of Queen Anne's lace and some tall purple flowers Gwen couldn't identify.

"Don't go near the water," Gwen called. She sat up, reminding herself that Tessie was too little to be trusted. The stream was shallow and slow-moving, but a child could lose her balance, fall, and hit her head on a rock.

"Be careful," she warned again, suddenly aware of how much Tessie meant to her. My instant sister, she scoffed at herself, but it was no joke. Tessie's giggles, her chatter, her eagerness to please were what had made the last few days bearable.

"I'm okay," Tessie called and headed back toward the willows. She sang to herself as she darted from one patch of flowers to another.

After a moment Gwen rested on her elbows and admired the view in front of her. Gradually she became aware of something odd. Except for Tessie's song, she could hear nothing at all — no birdsong, no buzzing insects. The stream rippled over the stones without a sound. Then Tessie's song grew more distant and stopped.

Gwen felt as if her heart had stopped beating, too. She wanted to call out, but the silence seemed unbreakable. As she stared, the peaceful setting around her broke apart like a jigsaw puzzle. The sky turned yellow-gray, and a strong wind flattened the wildflowers and the tall grass.

Huddled on her rock, unable to move, Gwen saw, not more than twenty feet away, a boat bouncing against the riverbank. Two men were in it, one young, one middle-aged, both dark-haired. The younger man was pushing against the bank with an oar, trying to move the boat out into the water. The older man pulled on a rope to start the boat's motor.

Gwen shook her head, trying to banish the vision that filled her eyes. She turned again to look up the bank. Tessie was gone. The wind whipped the willow branches so wildly that for a moment she missed the movement at the foot of one of the trees. Then she saw that someone was hiding there, peering around the trunk at the scene below. It was the ghost-girl, her eyes wide and full of fear, her long hair lifting in the gale.

" — peanut butter?" Tessie's piercing voice broke through the wall of silence. The sunlight was back; the girl was gone. Gwen stared at the quiet little stream where a boat had rocked and pounded seconds before.

"Do you want egg salad or peanut butter?" Tessie repeated. "I'm hungry."

Gwen threw her arms around the little girl and pulled her close. "Are you all right? Where did you go?"

"Didn't go anywhere," Tessie said, wriggling free. "I picked millions of flowers while you were sleeping." She waved a hand at the pile of Queen Anne's lace lying next to the rocks. "These are all for you."

But I wasn't sleeping! Gwen protested. What she'd just witnessed had been far too real to be a dream. The rushing river, the men, the girl had been there, if only for a moment.

She picked up the armful of flowers and buried her face in them. "Maybe I *did* doze off," she said as casually as possible. "You know what? I actually thought I saw a boat — right there!" She pointed at the bank in front of them. "That's pretty crazy, huh?"

Tessie giggled. "No boat," she said. "Never, never! This is just a little river, Gwennie."

And so it was. Standing at the water's edge, Gwen admitted to herself that a boat — any boat — would rest squarely on the rocky bottom. What she had seen was impossible, and yet she could recall every detail — the furious activity in the boat, the desperation in the men's faces, and, most of all, the look in the ghost-girl's eyes.

She feels all alone, Gwen thought, like me. And she's really scared. That's like me, too.

Chapter Six

"Go to Jail!" Dena groaned. "Why does that happen to me all the time? I'm a decent, law-abiding woman." She and Gwen were playing Monopoly at the dining room table, while Frank read the evening paper across from them and Tessie sat on the floor dressing and undressing her favorite doll. Only Jason was missing; as usual, he had gone upstairs as soon as dinner was over.

"You *look* decent and law-abiding," Frank teased. "But Justice is blind, you know."

Dena wrinkled her nose at him. She seemed relaxed, her depressed mood banished. Gwen was glad she'd said nothing about what had happened at the river that afternoon. What was the use? She'd tried to talk to Dena about the ghost-girl before and had been told the girl was just a dream. Dena would certainly say the same thing again; she might even question whether Gwen was a dependable sitter for Tessie.

"How about you, Gwen?" Frank asked suddenly. "Are you settling in okay?"

"I guess so. Tessie is showing me around." Gwen knew she sounded less than enthusiastic, but she couldn't help it. What would Frank say if she tried to tell him about this afternoon? He'd think I was crazy, she told herself. Ghosts and strange visions weren't a part of Frank's world. She knew that without being told.

Frank didn't seem to notice her hesitation. "Jason's the one who should be showing you around," he said, "instead of hiding out in his room."

Dena straightened the piles of fake money ranged in front of her. "He's not hiding out," she said. "He's working on his play. You know that."

"His play!" Frank snorted. "What kind of *work* is that for a teenaged kid during his summer vacation? He should be with people his own age."

"That's not so easy, living out here," Dena said mildly. "He doesn't have friends nearby."

"Well, then, he could be doing chores around

the place. Washing windows. Painting the barn. Why is it I have to *beg* him when I want something done?"

Dena looked up, and for a moment she seemed to be hiding a smile. Gwen almost laughed, too. The idea of Frank Mercy begging for anything was pretty funny. He didn't beg; he ordered.

"I've a good mind to go up there right now and tell him to come down here and act like a member of the family."

"No, don't!" Dena looked alarmed. "Don't start another fight tonight, Frank — I can't bear it." Sudden tears glistened in her eyes.

Frank gave in. "Have it your way," he said. "But that kid's turning into a real loner, and it's not good for him. You'll see."

Gwen thought Frank was probably right, but she felt sorry for Jason, too. She was fascinated to learn he was writing a play. He must be very smart — a genius, maybe. And geniuses were different from other people.

"What's the play for?" she asked, wondering if it was a dumb question. "I never knew a writer before."

Frank muttered under his breath, but Dena looked at her gratefully. "His English teacher thinks he has real talent. She promised that if he wrote a play this summer — and it was good —

she'd try to get the Drama Club to produce it this fall. Imagine what an honor that would be!" Her glowing expression said she could imagine it very easily.

"He'd be better off if he joined a softball team," Frank grumbled. "I'd let him take the car into town for *that*. I don't see why he has to run in to the library or the hardware store two or three times a week."

This was clearly a reference to some earlier argument. Gwen listened with interest and was sorry when Dena brought the conversation to an abrupt end.

"It's your turn, Gwen. I'm stuck here in Jail." She didn't look at her husband again, and after a moment or two, he went back to his newspaper.

At eight Tessie was taken upstairs to bed, and then the Monopoly game continued. Gwen wished it could last all night; she dreaded the hours ahead. Maybe I'll stay up and write my letter to Greg, she thought. Maybe I'll write a whole stack of letters and mail one of them every day. That'll impress him.

She moved her game piece along the board and thought about how strange it was to have to try to impress your own brother. Aunt Mary always said you should fight for what you wanted, but Gwen wished she didn't have to fight for Greg's attention. She'd do it if she had to, but she didn't like it.

Still, when the first letter was finished, well after midnight, she was pleased with it. She'd finally decided to say nothing at all about Mercy Manor being haunted; instead she had tried to let Greg know what he was missing by making her stay in Winfield.

. . . I don't have much to do here — just a few chores, which are easy for me because Aunt Mary taught me all about keeping house and I love it. I love to cook, too, but Dena does the cooking, so I don't have a chance. I really miss it. Aunt Mary let me make dinner a couple of times a week, and that was FUN. Cooking and cleaning are two of my favorite things. . . . She wondered if she was pressing too hard. But she had to make sure they understood. Surely Liz would welcome a houseguest who was eager to help.

I'll just keep telling them that in every letter, she decided. She tucked the letter into an envelope and undressed slowly, putting off as long as possible the moment when there would be nothing to think about except a ghost-girl prowling the hall just outside her door.

Maybe the girl was haunting the riverbank now; Gwen hoped so. She closed her eyes, and at once the scene at the river came back so vividly that she cowered under the covers. For the hundredth time, she wondered who the two men in the boat could be and why the girl was watching them.

I'm going to be awake all night, she thought miserably. And right after that she fell sound asleep, without a creak, a footstep, or a bad dream to disturb her for the rest of the night.

When she went downstairs the next morning, Jason was alone in the kitchen. Through the window, Gwen saw Dena busy at the clothesline and Tessie playing nearby.

"My dad says I should drive you into town if you want to go. What do you say?" Jason looked at her hopefully.

Gwen hesitated. Julie wouldn't be home for a long time, and there wasn't anyone else in Winfield she was ready to see right now.

"I guess I could look around the mall for a while," she said slowly. "If you don't have anything else to do."

"I'll go to the library." He smiled, and she was surprised again at how the smile changed his looks. "You can stay at the mall as long as you want."

Dena seemed pleased when she heard their

plans. "Do you need some money, Gwen?" she asked. "We must decide on an allowance for you."

"My brother gave me twenty dollars before he left," Gwen told her. "I haven't spent any of it."

"Well, that was thoughtful of him, wasn't it?" Dena patted her shoulder. "But you're still going to need an allowance. We'll talk to Frank."

"If you're handing out money — " Jason extended his hand, but his mother just laughed.

"I don't think your allowance is likely to grow until the barn gets painted," she said. "Your father has made that pretty clear."

"Clear enough," Jason muttered. "But I could use some money now."

"I can lend you some," Gwen offered impulsively.

After a quick glance at his mother, Jason shook his head. "I'll manage," he said. "Let's get going if we're going to go."

The trip to town began in silence, with Gwen full of questions waiting to be asked.

"What kind of play are you writing?" she asked, when it became clear that he wasn't going to start a conversation. "Or is it a secret?"

"It's not a secret." Jason sounded annoyed, then seemed to decide she was genuinely interested. "I'm writing about some kids in high school who get into trouble. Mrs. Sampson — she's my English teacher — she says writers should write about what they know. Especially young ones."

"Are you going to send it to a big Broadway producer when it's finished?"

Jason rolled his eyes. "Of course not. What Broadway producer is going to look at a high school kid's play? But there are some contests I can enter. And Mrs. Sampson says if it's good enough she'll get the Drama Club to put it on at school."

"That's what your mom told me. I just thought — "

"I'd rather have it produced in school than on Broadway," Jason said soberly. "My dad isn't the only one who thinks I'm a nerd."

Gwen decided that was probably true. She knew the boys in her class weren't interested in writing plays. And they certainly wouldn't understand someone who chose to spend his summer vacation writing one.

"I meant it about lending you some money," Gwen said after a moment. She wondered if he needed typewriter ribbons or paper for his play.

Jason shook his head. "My folks wouldn't like it. Besides," he added, "I'll make the stuff I need if I can't buy it."

Gwen waited, but he didn't explain, and she

decided she'd asked enough questions. A few minutes later they turned into the mall parking lot, and Jason let her out at the main door. "How long?" he asked.

"Is an hour okay?" When he looked disappointed, she decided she could always stop for a Coke and read a magazine. "Two hours, then."

"Sounds good." He was gone before she reached the door.

Once inside the mall, the two hours stretched out endlessly before her. She and Julie had come here nearly every Saturday during the school year. They seldom bought anything, but looking had been fun. It wasn't nearly as much fun when you did it alone. Gwen wandered in and out of their favorite stores, hesitating over a top here, a headband there, and deciding each time she didn't really want them. She had reached one end of the mall and was starting back on the other side when someone called her name.

"Gwen! Hi!"

It was Sandy Barber, a girl who'd sat next to her in social studies class last semester.

"Somebody said you'd moved out west after — oh, I'm sorry about your aunt." Sandy's brown eyes were bright with curiosity.

"Thanks." Gwen hesitated, then plunged into an explanation before Sandy could ask where she was living now. "I'm moving to Phoenix in a little while. I'm just staying with — with some friends of my aunt's until my brother and his wife find a bigger apartment." She took a deep breath. "They only have one bedroom now." She wondered if that was true and decided it wasn't. Greg would have said so when he was explaining why he couldn't take her with him.

"Phoenix." Sandy sounded impressed. "I've heard it's awfully hot there."

"We'll have air-conditioning." Gwen was surprised at how easy it was to make up a story. It felt wicked, but it was easy.

"Well, maybe I'll see you again before you go," Sandy suggested. "I know — we can have a sort of farewell party! I'll invite some kids from school."

Gwen felt as if a trap had snapped shut around her. Lying wasn't so easy after all. "I don't think I can," she said hastily. "I'm going to be pretty busy. And besides, my aunt's friends live out in the country, so it's hard for me to get into town." She saw Sandy's expression change and hurried on. "I'm just here today because they had some errands to do, and I didn't want to tag along."

"That's okay." Sandy turned to the counter next to her and examined the display of barrettes and headbands. "Have a good trip."

"Thanks." Gwen realized she'd sounded ungrateful, but she couldn't think of anything more to say. How could there be a farewell party when, so far at least, she wasn't going anywhere?

"Well, good-bye then."

Sandy didn't answer. They moved apart, and a moment later Gwen escaped from the store and started back down the mall. Her face was hot, and she had to struggle to keep herself from running. What would Aunt Mary say if she'd heard all those lies?

I could have told the truth, she thought bitterly. Sandy would have felt sorry for me, and she would tell everyone else, and they'd feel sorry for me, too.

She hurried on, sickened at the idea, knowing that if she met another of her classmates today she would lie all over again.

Chapter Seven

During the week that followed, Gwen sent three more letters to Phoenix. In each of them she mentioned how much she missed her cooking and cleaning chores, and how bored she was this summer. She felt guilty writing that she was bored — that was another lie. It was true that sometimes the days dragged, but there was always exploring to do with Tessie, and she'd discovered a whole bookcase of novels in the living room.

Talking with Dena was fun, too, as long as the conversation didn't touch on ghosts. Dena remembered exactly how it had felt to be not-quite-thirteen and transferring to a new school. She knew how embarrassing it was to have to dress differently from her friends. (Dena's mother had disapproved of shorts; Aunt Mary had hated blue jeans.) It occurred to Gwen during one of their long chats that Dena was about the age her own mother would have been if she had lived. She and her mother probably would have traded memories and laughed together just as she and Dena were doing now.

Still, in spite of the talks and the books, in spite of having the little sister she'd always longed for, Gwen wanted Greg to admit he'd been wrong to leave her in Winfield. Each morning she waited anxiously for the mail-carrier's blue sedan to turn into the backyard, but at the end of the week there was still no letter from Phoenix. On Saturday a postcard arrived from Julie with a picture of the Rocky Mountains. *Miss you*, it said. *I hope you're having fun. Don't ever go on a car trip with little brothers.*

The ghost-girl didn't return, though Gwen listened tensely each night until she fell asleep. Gradually the memory of the two men in the boat and their frightened observer faded, until she was almost able to convince herself that Tessie had been right. Maybe she *had* fallen asleep on the riverbank and had had a bad dream.

One afternoon, watching her study the rows of titles in the bookcase, Dena said, "There are more books in the basement, Gwen. Boxes full of them, in fact. Come on, I'll show you."

Together, they went down the stairs into a shadowy cavern Gwen hadn't visited before. The washer and dryer were close to the foot of the steps. Beyond them, a hanging bulb spread a thin pool of light in the center of the room. The huge bulk of the furnace loomed in one corner, and stacks of boxes leaned against the walls.

"What's that?" Gwen narrowed her eyes at a rectangular shape that towered above the boxes along the furnace wall.

Dena followed her stare. "It's a grandfather clock — my father built it. It wasn't working when we moved, so Frank took out the insides and packed them separately. The books are over there." She pointed to the far wall where two piles of boxes and crates stood next to a wooden door. "The crates are full of pictures and linens and knickknacks, all kinds of things from our house in town. I keep telling myself I must unpack them, but then I think, maybe we won't stay here forever, and I'll just have to pack them up again." She had begun to sound uneasy, as if the dreary basement had affected her mood.

If that was true, Gwen could understand why. There was a heaviness in the air. She found herself stealing quick glances over her shoulder and peering into corners to make sure no one was lurking there.

They dragged a couple of boxes into the pool of light.

"There are mysteries in this one," Dena announced. "Do you like mysteries?"

"Sure." Gwen hurriedly chose a half-dozen books and then turned to the second box.

"Those are biographies — my favorites," Dena told her. "I think I'll take some upstairs and start reading them all over again."

When they had made their choices, they stacked the books on the steps and pushed the boxes back against the wall. Gwen dusted off her hands, discovering as she straightened that she was standing beside the wooden door.

"What's in here? A fruit cellar?"

Suddenly Dena was impatient. "No! Well, it was. But now it's just an empty room. Look for yourself."

"It doesn't matter," Gwen protested, but Dena brushed past her and threw open the door. She reached inside and found the light switch.

Gwen looked around, wondering what it was about the fruit cellar that could have made Dena so irritable. The room was small, with two walls lined with shelves. A table stood against a third wall. The only unusual thing was the fact that, while the whole basement had only one hanging bulb to light it, the little room had two, one in the center of the ceiling and one above the table.

"Maybe this used to be a workroom," Gwen said. "Could it have been your uncle's?"

"I have no idea." Dena backed out of the room, one hand on the switch. "Let's get out of here. I don't like this basement. I even hate doing the wash down here. If we stay, Frank is going to have to add a laundry room upstairs."

They closed the wooden door, gathered up the books they had selected, and scurried up the stairs. Gwen felt the tightness seep out of her shoulders as she closed the basement door behind them.

Dena's mood changed again, too. She smiled at Gwen apologetically. "Sorry if I was snappish down there. I didn't mean to be, but there's something about that place. . . ."

Gwen nodded. "It's sort of depressing," she agreed. "Is that why you don't like this house anymore?"

Dena didn't meet her eyes. "Of course not. I do like it — most of the time, anyway. It's just that I don't — I don't know what's best for all of us." She gave a forced little laugh and shrugged the question away. "I'm going to start dinner."

"Can I help?" Gwen wanted to hear more, but Dena waved her toward the back door.

"If you'll just track down Tessie, that's all the help I need," she said. "She's usually good about staying in the yard, but you never know."

That evening Jason remained downstairs with the family. Gwen wondered if he'd been warned by his mother that there would be another explosion if he continued to disappear into his bedroom as soon as dinner was over. He had a book in his lap and seldom looked up from it, but Frank seemed pleased to have him there.

Dena sat quietly with a stack of mending at her side, and Gwen and Tessie cuddled on the couch reading Tessie's "most best" books. Reading to Tessie was something Gwen enjoyed. She changed her voice for every character — roaring, squealing, growling, hissing — and was rewarded with delighted giggles.

"I love you, Gwennie," Tessie confided, when they had reached the last page of the last book in the pile. "You're funny."

For a moment, Gwen couldn't answer. Then, "I love you, too," she said softly and gave the little girl a hug. Tessie was wonderful, solid, real. Sitting next to her, it was possible to forget, for a while at least, about the ghost-girl and the vision at the riverbank.

When she went up to her room an hour later, the paper rose was lying on her bedside table.

Gwen stood in the doorway staring, as if she could make the flower go away if she looked at it hard enough. Down the hall, she could hear Dena and Frank talking in their bedroom.

I ought to call them right now — show them! But show them what? The rose was harmless, a fold of red construction paper. Dena would either laugh or scold, and Frank would wonder what the fuss was about. It's a present from Tessie, he'd say. Why all the excitement? And he would look at her the same way he looked at Jason, as if she were beyond all understanding.

She hesitated a moment longer, then picked up the rose and dropped it into the bottom dresser drawer with her sweaters and scarves. Out of sight, out of mind, she told herself, but she doubted Aunt Mary's old saying would hold true tonight. The presence of the rose seemed a warning of something about to happen.

It took a long time for the house to settle into quiet. June bugs rattled against the screens, and the curtains swayed in the breeze. Gwen stared into the darkness. If there was one thing she'd remember about Mercy Manor, she thought, it would be the waiting.

When the sound began, as she'd been sure it would, it was so soft that at first she doubted her ears. She threw back the sheet and stood up, feeling for her slippers with her toes. The rustling sound became footsteps. They were just outside her door, or perhaps at Tessie's door across the hall.

She tiptoed across the floor and peeked out. At first the hall seemed totally dark, but as she stared through the opening, a light shimmered and gathered strength at the top of the back stairs. A figure shaped itself in the light, the straight-backed figure of a young girl with long blonde hair. Gwen opened her door a little more, and the girl looked over her shoulder with frightened eyes, then held out her hand in a pleading gesture.

She wants me to follow her.

Trembling, Gwen stepped into the hall. The girl was partway down the stairs now, her blonde hair shining. At the curve of the steps she looked back again, as if to make sure Gwen was coming. Then she went on, and the light vanished around the curve.

Gwen stepped into the deep well of darkness at the top of the stairs. I can't do this! she told herself, panic-stricken. Her chest ached so she could hardly breathe, and she felt as if her feet were moving down the steps without her willing it. When she reached the curve, the light appeared again, a gentle glow in which the figure of the girl came and went. At the bottom of the stairs it drifted into the kitchen. Then, to Gwen's horror, it moved back into the hall, to the basement door.

"No!" She said the word aloud, in a kind of strangled gasp. She couldn't follow the ghost to the basement. Thoughts of this afternoon, the musty, suffocating atmosphere, the suspicion of something lurking, swept over her. As the girl waited at the basement door, she turned and stumbled back up the stairs.

"Gwen! What in the world . . ." Dena stood at the door of the master bedroom, her hand on the light switch. "What are you doing?"

"N-Nothing."

"What do you mean, nothing? You've been downstairs — were you hungry?" Dena hurried down the hall to Gwen's bedroom and drew her inside. "Let's not wake up the whole house."

Gwen moved numbly. She supposed she could say she'd gone downstairs for a snack, but she was too frightened to pretend. The ghost-girl was real; this time Dena had to believe. She turned on the little lamp over her bed. "It was that girl —

do you remember I told you I saw a girl in the hallway one night? A girl with long blonde hair?"

"I remember." Dena's voice sharpened the way it had in the basement that afternoon. "But you were dreaming, Gwen. I can't see why you keep thinking about it."

"I didn't dream it. I didn't! I saw her again just now. She was right here! First I heard her out in the hall, and then I followed her down the steps. She went into the basement."

Dena stepped backward as if she'd been slapped. "This is absolutely ridiculous!" she said. "There's no reason to make up stories. . . ." She shook her head. "Maybe you're still upset about your aunt's death — that would be understandable. But your dreams and reality are all mixed up."

"I wasn't asleep," Gwen insisted. "I was just lying here listening, and pretty soon I heard footsteps. I guessed the girl was going to come again because she left the rose. . . ." She went to the dresser and pulled out the bottom drawer. The paper rose was gone.

"She left *what*?"

"A flower. A rose. It's gone now, but it was on the table when I came up to bed. She left it here once before. Tessie says she's left it in her room, too."

"Now that *is* nonsense." Dena sounded outraged, but Gwen guessed this wasn't the first time she'd heard about the rose. Tessie must have talked about seeing the girl, too, and had been told she was mistaken. "I'm sure I don't know what it is you think you saw," she went on, "but I hope you'll be able to ignore it. You mustn't worry the rest of the family. Particularly Tessie."

"I'd never scare Tessie," Gwen said quickly. "But I thought you ought to know."

"All right." Dena wrapped her robe around her and moved toward the door. "Now you've told me, so let's forget it. No more prowling around in the middle of the night without turning on the light, promise? You could have fallen downstairs."

"Okay."

The door opened and closed, and Gwen was alone. She leaned back on her pillow and pulled the sheet up to her chin. For a long time she lay taut and sick, reliving those terrifying moments on the stairs and Dena's refusal to talk about them.

Aunt Mary would say, People can't change the truth by denying it. Gwen wished she could talk to her great-aunt right now. She'd ask her what a person could do if she *knew* what the truth was and couldn't make anyone else believe it?

Chapter Eight

Wednesday, a.m.

Dear Gwen,

I never guessed you'd be such an enthusiastic letter-writer! It's good to hear from you, but I hope you won't mind if I don't answer every letter. We've been busy here, and I don't have much time for writing.

I didn't know you enjoyed housekeeping so much either. Tell Mrs. Mercy how you feel, and I'm sure she'll find some more chores for you to do. She doesn't want to feel she's taking advantage of you, and that's why she hesitates to ask you to do things.

I envy you, living in the country. Phoenix is blazingly hot — be glad you don't have to stay indoors close to the air-conditioning.

Liz says hello. She's been shopping for furniture, and she's having a lot of fun trying out new recipes. I'm glad *to let her experiment on me, because so far the results have been delicious.*

Take care of yourself, and make the most of your summer vacation.

Love,
Greg

Gwen read the letter three times. She was looking for some hint that her brother was sorry she wasn't with them in Phoenix, but each reading made her more certain he wasn't sorry in the least. He had told her she should be grateful to be in Wisconsin instead of Arizona. And he wanted her to understand that Liz was a good cook who enjoyed making their meals herself and didn't need any help. Obviously, he wasn't thinking about inviting Gwen to join them, and he didn't want her to think about it either.

She crumpled the letter and threw herself on the bed, close to tears. This was it then — the moment she'd dreaded ever since the afternoon of Aunt Mary's funeral, and even before. Till now, she had been able to convince herself that Greg just needed time to reconsider. He would realize they should be together. Now the cool, offhand tone of his letter told her, once and for all, that he didn't want her.

But I can't stay here! She stared into the mirror

over the dresser, imagining night after sleepless night with the ghost-girl outside her bedroom door. . . . *Someone has to listen to me.*

A door opened and closed, and Jason's footsteps sounded in the hall. Gwen stood up and smoothed her hair. She'd promised not to frighten Tessie, but she hadn't said she wouldn't talk to Jason. Maybe he had seen the phantom himself and hadn't told his parents. He'd know they wouldn't believe him.

She stepped out into the hall, nearly colliding with Jason. He was wearing ragged jeans, a shapeless T-shirt, and an expression so grim that she almost changed her mind about confiding in him.

"If you want to go to town, I can't," he said bluntly. "I have to start painting the barn today."

"I don't want to go to town," Gwen retorted. "I want to tell you something. It's important."

He eyed her curiously. "Hey, have you been crying?"

Gwen shrugged the question away. "Just listen to me," she begged. "It won't take long."

He leaned against the wall, elaborately patient. "Go ahead."

Keeping her voice at a whisper, Gwen told him about the ghost-girl. "She keeps coming back, and she acts as if she wants me to follow her —

she came again last night. And she goes down the steps to the basement. Sometimes she leaves a paper rose in my room. I think she's left it in Tessie's room, too — at least, Tessie says so."

Jason's expression, intent at first, became skeptical as he listened. He laughed when she mentioned the rose. "I bet you read a lot of ghost stories," he said. "I bet you love 'em."

Gwen glared at him. "What if I do?" she demanded. "That doesn't mean I'm making up this one. It all happened — everything I've told you."

Jason shook his head. "No, it didn't. There isn't any blonde girl in this house — you're imagining the whole thing. I bet you never lived in a creaky old place like this before."

"Have you?" She hated his know-it-all expression.

"Sure have. Our house in town wasn't as big as this one, but it was just as old. And it was creaky as blazes. Creaky doesn't mean a thing."

"That's what your mother said," Gwen told him icily. "But I saw the girl. Three times."

"You thought you saw someone. My advice is to forget the whole crazy business."

It was almost exactly what Dena had told her to do a few hours before. Gwen had been hurt then, but now she was furious. Jason was only a few years older than she was, but he was treating her as if she were a silly baby. She whirled and went back into her bedroom, slamming the door behind her.

There was a pause, then a knock. "Hey. What's the big deal?"

As if he cared!

"Come on, Gwen."

She waited, fists clenched, till she heard him go downstairs, heavy-footed with annoyance. He was probably afraid she'd tell his father he'd been rude to her. Well, let him worry. She was through trying to tell the Mercy family anything.

Half an hour later there was another knock at the door. This time it was Dena, with Tessie at her side.

"We just had a great idea," she said with determined cheerfulness. "I don't have anything special to do today. Let's go to Winfield and pick out a rug for your bedroom. Wouldn't that be fun? We can have lunch in town."

"And ice cream," Tessie said. "Come on, Gwennie."

Gwen put down the book she'd been trying to read. "Okay," she said. "If you want to. But I don't mind the floor the way it is."

"Well, I do," Dena said. "And I'd like your help in choosing something to cover it." She took Tessie's hand and swung her around toward the hall. "We'll tell Jason we're going, and we'll meet you at the car."

When they were gone, Gwen crossed to the dresser and began brushing her hair in front of the mirror. She looked the same, but she wasn't. She felt as if Greg's letter and the conversation with Jason had turned her into — what was Aunt Mary's word? — a loner. A loner was someone like Miss Crockett, who lived in a big house on Barker Drive and didn't come out except to do her shopping on Wednesday mornings. Or like Mr. Grace, who walked the Winfield streets all day, talking to himself and never meeting anyone's eyes. Loners didn't need other people; they had learned to take care of themselves.

She gave her hair a final swipe, straightened her shoulders, lifted her chin — and shivered. It was easy to look like a person who could take care of herself, but a lot harder to feel like one.

Dena was already in the car, and Tessie was at the foot of the ladder watching Jason apply red paint to the side of the barn.

"I'll help you when we come home," she offered. "I'll do the bottom part."

Jason rolled his eyes at the thought and grinned down at Gwen, but she pretended not to notice. Silently, she climbed into the backseat of the station wagon, leaving the front for Tessie, and fastened the seatbelt.

"It's a great day for painting," Dena said. "Not too hot." She leaned out the window and called Tessie to the car. "We'll be back around mid-afternoon," she told Jason. "There's a pitcher of lemonade in the fridge."

He lifted a hand to show he'd heard and went back to his painting. He was a hard worker when he finally got started on a job, Gwen admitted grudgingly. He cut the grass with care, trimming around every tree and bush, and he was a con-scientious gardener. He was probably just as par-ticular about the play he was writing, laboring over every line. But even if that was all true, it didn't change the fact that he was self-centered and rude and not in the least concerned about other people's feelings.

Dena and Tessie chattered all the way into Winfield, occasionally directing a comment to Gwen, forcing her to take part in the conver-sation.

"What did your brother have to say in his let-ter?" Dena asked as they approached the out-skirts of the town. "Is he well?"

"He's all right." Gwen tried to think of some-thing she could report witout giving away her disappointment at the contents of the letter. "It's hot in Phoenix. And they're buying furniture."

"Just like we are," Dena commented. "I think we should look for a desk for your room, too. You're going to need one when school starts."

It was nearly noon when they turned onto Winfield's main street. Dena parked in the lot next to Carolyn's Café, saying they might as well eat before they started their shopping. Tessie was delighted, and all through their lunch of hamburgers, fries, and salad, she kept changing her mind about what kind of sundae she wanted for dessert. Strawberries on mint ice cream was the final decision. The waitress looked doubtful, but Tessie ate every bite and looked hungrily at the chocolate sundaes the others had ordered.

"Now we're ready to get to work," Dena said briskly, when the last spoonful was swallowed and the bill paid. "The Carpet Mart is just across the street. We'll start there, and if we don't find something we like, we'll go to the mall."

The Carpet Mart was a long, brightly lit room, with two aisles running between stacks of carpet rolls. Dena turned down one aisle with Tessie trotting behind her, and Gwen took the other side. She could see a display of braided rag rugs near the back of the store and was drawn to it, thinking of Tessie's "perfect" bedroom. Not that I care, she reminded herself. It's just a room I have to sleep in for a while. She looked up at the big rug that hung on the wall with smaller rugs mounted on either side. It was oval in shape, and the colors — rose, pink, lavender, and white — seemed to glow. She could picture it on the bedroom floor, lit by the morning sun.

"That's the one, isn't it?" Dena had come around the end of the stack of carpets and was watching Gwen's face with amusement. "It's really beautiful. Just right."

"Yes, it is!" Gwen forgot to sound indifferent. "Those are my favorite colors."

Dena squinted at the price tag tacked next to the rug. "Right you are!" she exclaimed. "A just-right rug and a bargain besides." She turned toward the saleswoman who was coming down the aisle.

"We'd like that one," she said, pointing. "If you don't mind breaking up your display."

The saleswoman, gray-haired and talkative, seemed genuinely delighted to hear that they had found exactly what they wanted. "I love to see people pleased with their purchases!" she told them. "This is just a part-time job for me, to keep busy, you know. Every time I make a sale, I'm glad I didn't decide to sit at home and grow old in my retirement years." She took a sales pad from the pocket of her smock and started writing.

"What did you do before you retired?" Dena asked politely.

"I was a social worker," the woman replied. "And let me tell you, it wasn't easy. I saw a lot of sadness in my work. That's why I enjoy seeing my customers happy and satisfied now." She took Dena's name and address and went back to the service desk to arrange for the delivery of the rug.

Gwen shifted from one foot to the other. Her pleasure in finding the rug was already beginning to fade. She wasn't a happy, satisfied customer, she thought. She was a scared one. And a loner.

When the clerk returned, she wore a puzzled expression. "For some reason your address sounds familiar to me," she said. "Not your name, just the address. It's out in the country north of town, isn't it?"

Dena nodded.

"Then I think — I think I may have been there. Many, many years ago. It was one of my first calls after I moved to Winfield, and I got lost looking for the house. That's why the address stayed in my mind, I suppose. I can't think what it was that took me there. . . ." She looked at Dena expectantly.

Dena bent to sign the sales slip. "We've been there only a couple of years," she said, and Gwen heard the sudden coolness in her voice. "I grew up here in town."

"Oh, well, then." The clerk shook her head. "My memory isn't what it used to be. Seems to me there was something about a runaway — "

"I wouldn't know anything about it." This time Dena's tone was so chilly that the saleswoman looked startled. She smiled uncertainly, gave Dena the sales slip, and followed them to the door with assurances that the rug would be delivered the next day.

They crossed the street and climbed into the station wagon. Dena turned the key in the ignition and sat staring straight ahead as if she'd forgotten what to do next.

"The mall, Mama," Tessie prompted. "You said we could go there."

"We're going — don't whine." Gwen had a clear view of the rearview mirror and Dena's face. She was disturbed about something, no mistake about that, but she struggled to smile at Tessie. "We'll look for a desk for Gwen. That'll be fun, won't it?"

"I'm going to look for toys," Tessie said. "That'll be more fun."

Maybe the social worker came the summer Dena stayed at Mercy Manor with her aunt and uncle, Gwen thought. If that were true, would

Dena remember it? She had been only five at the time, but she remembered other things about that summer — dancing in the light of the stained-glass window, hiding in the nooks and corners of the big house. Would she be aware of something unusual enough to bring a social worker to Mercy Manor?

Gwen studied her foster-mother's expression in the mirror and knew she'd get no answers to her questions. She thought of calm, never-moody Aunt Mary and tried to guess what she'd say about Dena Mercy.

Poor girl — she has more ups and downs than a roller coaster.

Chapter Nine

"I want you to use it, Gwen. My mother made it for Tessie, but she's much too young to appreciate it." Dena folded the quilt that had covered Gwen's bed and in its place spread a new pink sheet. Over that went a delicate coverlet of crocheted flowers and foliage. "The pink is beautiful with this rug. Now there's one more touch. . . ." She crossed the room and hurried down the hall to her own bedroom at the front of the house.

Left alone, Gwen looked around her with mixed feelings. The bedroom, so bare and impersonal when she saw it first, had become her own. The oval rug was as warm and bright as she'd thought it would be, and there was a bouquet of Queen Anne's lace, picked by Tessie, on the brand-new kneehole desk. And now the bedspread! Gwen could tell from the way Dena handled it that it was precious. Everything in the room told her that the Mercys cared about her and wanted her with them. But not enough to listen, she thought miserably. Not enough to believe me when I tell them something important.

Dena returned carrying three small pastel pillows. "Here's what I did last night," she said proudly, "while you and Tessie were reading her dinosaur books. They're old pillows, but I had some scraps of pink and lavender big enough to make new covers." She arranged the pillows on the bed and stood back to admire the effect. "What do you think?"

"They look really pretty," Gwen said. "Thanks a lot, Dena — for the bedspread, too. I'll take good care of it."

"I'm sure you will." Dena hesitated. "You know, I just remembered some flower prints from the old house — they're in a box in the basement. They'd be just right over the head of the bed."

"It doesn't matter," Gwen said quickly.

Dena shrugged. "We'll see," she said. "What are you going to do this morning?"

"Answer Greg's letter, I guess."

Dena bent to adjust one of the new pillows. "I have to do a couple of loads of laundry," she said, and a shadow crossed her face. "After you've written your letter, come down and keep me company. We can look for the prints together."

When she had gone, Gwen sat at the new desk and took her box of stationery from the top drawer. This was going to be a hard letter to write, but she had decided she must do it. Greg and Liz didn't want her to live with them, she knew that. But she had never told them about the ghost-girl. They didn't know how frightened she was. If they did, maybe there was still a chance they would reconsider.

. . . I'm trapped here, with scary stuff happening and no one who'll believe me! . . . I don't know why Tessie and I are the only people who see the ghost — maybe we aren't. But Dena won't talk about her or let me talk about her. Last night I was awake for hours. The ghost didn't come, but I was so scared she might that I felt sick the whole time. . . .

She read over what she had written, hating it and, at the same time, wondering if it sounded convincing. She was pretty sure she could never make Greg believe in ghosts, but he had to listen to her. He might sneer at her story, but that wouldn't matter if he understood that she had to get away.

There was one thing more to tell him. She chewed the tip of her pen, then finished the letter quickly.

. . . Please don't call Dena or anything like that. If she knew I told you, it would upset her very much.

She stuffed the sheet of paper into an envelope and carried the letter out to the mailbox before she could change her mind about sending it. Begging was humiliating; begging to go where you weren't wanted was worst of all. Only the thought of those long, dark hours of waiting and listening made her leave the letter in the box.

When she returned to the house, she filled a glass with water at the kitchen sink and stood sipping and listening to the sound of the washing machine downstairs. Through the window she could watch Tessie in her sandbox in the far corner of the yard, talking to herself and occasionally to Jason who was up on the ladder painting the barn doors. She was tempted to go out and help build a sand castle, but her conscience told her she ought to go down to the basement. Dena wanted her company. No matter how firmly her foster mother denied there was a ghost in the house, Gwen knew she didn't like being in the basement alone.

Dena, her face pale in the dim light, looked up from the socks she was sorting and smiled when she heard Gwen coming downstairs. "Have you finished your letter?" she called above the *thump-thump* of the machine.

Gwen nodded.

"I'm just waiting for this washerful to finish up — it's practically done — and then I'll put it in the drier and we'll look for those flower prints. They're over there, in one of those boxes in front of the grandfather clock."

Gwen peered into the shadows beyond the ring of light. For some reason, this second visit to the basement wasn't as disturbing as the first had been. The sound of the washing machine and the lemony smell of detergent reminded her of washday at Aunt Mary's house. She sat on the second step from the bottom and waited until the washing machine turned itself off.

"Finally," Dena said, her voice loud in the sudden silence.

"I'll fill the drier," Gwen offered. She worked fast, transferring the wet clothes while Dena went over to the stack of boxes near the furnace wall.

"These two big crates have the pictures in them." Dena said. "Someday I'll have to — "

The telephone shrilled upstairs. "Now, who could that be?" Dena came back to the steps and looked at Gwen. "Do you want to start going through the crates yourself? There's a vase full of roses and another of tulips. You can't miss them."

The telephone rang again, and she darted up the stairs. Gwen started after her and then stopped. If she left the basement now, she would be admitting that she didn't dare stay down there alone. Dena would know, and it might trigger another one of her mood changes.

She switched on the drier and rested a hand on it, reassured by the low, familiar hum. Dena would be right back. She would wait.

After a moment she crossed the basement and bent over one of the two large crates. It was full of framed pictures of all sizes stacked on end. She began taking them out, one at a time, looking briefly at landscapes and photographs and a faded painting of an old-fashioned garden. There was a pen-and-ink drawing of a sleepy St. Bernard dog, and another of two little boys sitting on a wide swing — but no vases of roses and tulips.

She shifted her knees and reached for the second crate, dragging it out and away from the grandfather clock. More photographs — an old lady wearing an apron, a young man posed proudly next to the cab of a truck. She pulled out a third photograph and caught her breath. There were two figures in this one: a dark-haired man seated on a straight-backed chair and, behind him, a much younger man. They were smiling and relaxed, but Gwen recognized them at once. She had seen them before in the boat at the riverbank.

As she stared, she became aware of a change in the basement. She could no longer hear the hum of the drier. The air had turned damp and musty. She started to scramble to her feet, but as she struggled, there was a movement above her. She looked up and saw the grandfather clock tilted forward, ready to fall.

Afterward, Gwen was never quite sure what had happened next. She remembered tumbling backward onto the concrete floor with the clock arcing down toward her, the carved peak above the dial pointing at her chest. Then there was a whirl of movement, a flash of gold, and a crash that seemed to shake the foundations of the house.

Footsteps raced down the basement stairs. The drier began to hum again. Dena was standing over her, looking down in horror.

"Gwen, are you all right? Oh, Gwen!"

Gwen sat up and stared at the clock lying at her side. "It fell," she said unnecessarily. "I'm sorry — maybe I bumped it when I moved the crate of pictures. I bet it's ruined."

Together they lifted the tall clock-case and shoved it back against the wall. The dial-cover and the glass pendulum case were shattered, but the wood was intact except for a long gouge on one side.

"Do you think it can be fixed?"

Dena's eyes were still wide with fright. "Of course it can. The important thing is that you're all right. If the clock had landed on top of you, it might have killed you!" She threw her arms around Gwen and hugged her. "When I heard that crash, I thought — I thought — I don't know what I thought!" She stepped back with a shaky laugh. "Oh, dear, I left Mrs. Adams on the line without a word of explanation. I'd better go back and see if she's still waiting."

"I'll come, too," Gwen said. "We can find the flower prints some other time."

"And clean up the broken glass," Dena said. "What a mess!" She pointed at a picture frame lying on its face. "That's probably broken, too."

Gwen bent and turned it over. The two men, one young, one middle-aged, grinned up at her through a webbing of cracks.

"Oh, that!" Dena took the photo from Gwen's numb fingers and looked at it with distaste. "We won't bother to have that glass replaced. The picture belonged to my parents, but I never hung it in our house in town."

"Why not?" Gwen asked. "Who are they?"

She tried to make the question casual.

Dena put the picture back on the floor and started for the stairs. "They're my uncle Raymond and my cousin Allen," she said. "They've both been dead for years. They lived in this house when I was a little girl." She turned back to Gwen with a frown. "You know, I honestly don't know why I dislike them so much. I never had much to do with either of them when I stayed here that summer, as far as I can remember. And Aunt Josie was wonderful. But the way it all turned out . . ." She shrugged as if the subject was painful. "I'd better get back to poor Mrs. Adams. Or call her and apologize. Come on."

"The way *what* turned out?" Gwen hurried up the stairs, but her steps slowed as she reached the top. It was no use. She knew Dena wouldn't finish that sentence.

Chapter Ten

"She could have been killed, Frank." Dena's voice was sharp. "You'd better bring the clock upstairs, even if you don't have time to fix it right now. It might fall again — I don't think the basement floor is level."

"I'll have a repairman come out and pick it up," Frank said. He cut another slice from the roast beef and looked around the table inquiringly. "Might as well have it put back in working condition. He can replace the glass, too."

"Gwen really could have been killed," Dena repeated. "It could have been terrible. . . ."

She seemed to be trying to convince herself as well as the rest of the family that what had happened in the basement that morning had been an accident. But how can she be so sure? Gwen wondered. I was close to the clock, but I didn't touch it — not enough to move it, anyway. She recalled the strange silence in the basement and the musty smell just before the clock fell. And what about that blur of movement — that brief glimpse of gold? It could have been the ghost-girl's hair. The more she thought about it, the more certain she was that she had actually seen the girl as the clock began to tip. She pushed it aside, Gwen told herself. The clock was going to fall on me, and she kept it from happening.

The ring of the telephone cut into her thoughts. Frank pushed back his chair and went out to the kitchen to answer. He was back almost at once, crooking a finger at Jason.

"For you — the assistant coach at the high school." He looked pleased and puzzled. "What does he want? I wonder."

Jason didn't looked pleased at all. "I can guess," he mumbled and went with dragging steps to take the call.

"What does that mean? He can guess?" Frank demanded. "Has the coach called him before?"

Dena looked anxious. "Not that I know of. When will you talk to someone about the clock, Frank?"

He put a finger to his lips. "Later," he whispered. "I want to hear this."

There was little to hear. Jason's side of the conversation consisted of "Uh-huh" and "I guess not" and "I won't have time," each repeated at least once. When he returned to the dining room, his face was flushed, and he kept his head down, avoiding their eyes.

"Well?" The word seemed to burst from Frank's lips. "What did he want?"

Jason sat down and spooned the last of his melted ice cream. "Wanted me to play on the basketball team this fall," he mumbled. "Same old thing."

Frank stared at him. "You mean he's asked you before?"

"Last semester." Jason raised his head. "It's just because I'm tall. And I made a few baskets in gym class."

"But that's great!" Frank exclaimed. "It's just what you need. My son the basketball star!" He slapped the table so hard they all jumped.

"I said no," Jason told him coldly. "Same as the last time."

There was a long silence while Frank digested this information. Even Tessie knew enough to keep quiet, though she looked as if she were bursting with questions.

"If he doesn't want to, Frank . . ." Dena began nervously.

"You had a special invitation to be on the basketball team, and you turned it down," Frank interrupted. "Half the boys at Winfield High would jump at the chance, but Jason Edward Mercy says no." He shook his head. "Same as the last time! Why is it I didn't hear about this before?"

"Because I knew what you'd say!" Jason exclaimed. "Just what you're saying now. I don't want to play basketball! They practice every night after school, and on weekends they travel all over the state. I've got things to do."

"Like what?" His father demanded. "What do you have to do that's so important you can't play basketball?"

Jason sent a desperate glance in his mother's direction, and for a moment Gwen felt sorry for him. Then she remembered how he'd laughed at her when she'd told him about the ghost-girl. Serves him right, she thought. He doesn't worry about anyone but himself.

"I want to write," Jason said. "And if Mrs. Sampson gets the Drama Club to produce my play, I want to be at all the rehearsals to see what happens. And if she says the play isn't good enough, I want to write another one and another one until I learn how to do it. I'm going to try some short stories and poetry, too." He paused for breath, then rushed on. "I know you don't think that stuff's important, but it is to me, Dad. A lot more important than a dumb old basketball game!" He turned away from his father's red-faced glare. "That's all I have to say," he finished lamely.

"You've said plenty," Frank snapped. "You're telling me you want to be a bookworm — a hermit! What am I supposed to do, cheer? A kid your age should be learning how to get along with people. There's a lot more to life than putting words on paper."

"I know that." Jason jumped up and pushed back his chair. "Let's forget the whole thing, okay? Just forget it." He stalked out of the dining room, through the kitchen, and out the back door, letting the screen slam behind him.

Gwen looked from Frank to Dena. They were both grim-faced, and Dena was close to tears.

"That kid!" Frank exploded. "I know what he thinks. He thinks I want him to get into sports just so I can brag about him."

"Maybe if you showed more interest in what he's writing," Dena said cautiously. "Mrs. Sampson says he's very talented."

Frank shook his head. "He doesn't need any more encouragement to do *that*. He can write if he wants to, but he'd better learn to do a few

91

other things, too, or he's going to be a hopeless misfit."

"What's a misfit?" Tessie demanded, unable to be still another minute. "What's a bookworm? Does it crawl into a book? Jason doesn't crawl into books." She looked so concerned that Dena smiled weakly and put out a comforting hand.

"You help me with the dishes," she suggested, "and I'll explain about bookworms. We'll give Gwen a vacation tonight."

When they had left the table, Gwen shifted uneasily in her chair. She wanted to leave, too, but Frank lingered, resting his chin in one big hand.

"You're getting a heavy dose of family life, aren't you?" he said after a while. "Must be pretty different from living with your aunt."

Gwen didn't know how to reply.

"I'm sorry about your accident this morning," Frank went on. "Better stay out of the basement as much as possible till we get things sorted down there. I'll find those prints you and Dena were looking for." He smiled tiredly, and Gwen thought again how much she liked him, even when he roared. Jason didn't know how lucky he was to have a father who cared.

Later in the evening she heard Jason come back into the house and slip quietly upstairs. Neither Frank nor Dena looked up from the television screen. Solemn-faced, they were watching a comedy Frank had brought home from the video store in Winfield. Gwen thought the film was funny, but the Mercys stared at it blankly, their thoughts clearly miles away. When the movie ended and a sports news program began, Gwen said good night, relieved to escape the tension that filled the living room.

In her bedroom, she undressed quickly, then hurried to the bathroom without bothering to turn on the hall light. On her way back, she stopped, aware that something was different. Ahead of her, the panel of light from her bedroom showed Tessie's closed door and, beyond it, the attic door slowly opening. As she stepped back against the wall, Jason moved into the light. He was carrying his shoes in one hand.

"Oh, it's you." He sounded relieved and annoyed at the same time. "I thought you were downstairs watching television."

"The movie's over." He was whispering, so she whispered, too. "What were you doing up in the attic?"

"Working on something," he said. "Don't mention it to my dad, okay?"

"Why should I?" Gwen didn't feel like doing him any favors, but she wasn't a tattletale either.

"Why shouldn't you be up there if you want to?"

He made an impatient gesture. "I just don't want him poking around. If he sees what I'm doing, he'll know how much time it's taken, and then he'll get mad all over again. You saw how he was at dinner. What he doesn't know won't hurt him."

"He just wants you to have a good life," Gwen said. "Why do you fight with him all the time?"

Jason ducked his head, and when he looked up again his eyes held the trace of a smile. "I've been wondering the same thing. What good does it do? I'm just not what he wants — I'm not a basketball star and I never will be."

"How do you know if you haven't tried?"

"Don't want to try." He started to brush past her, then turned back, the smile in full evidence. "You know what? I've finally figured something out. I am who I am — and I guess I'm not going to fall apart if everyone doesn't approve. Still," he paused, "you're not going to say anything about the attic, right?"

"I said I wouldn't tell," Gwen told him coolly. "Don't worry about it." She went into her bedroom with his words resounding in her ears.

"I am who I am . . . ," she whispered to herself in front of the mirror and began brushing her hair with short, hard strokes.

I'm a person who doesn't know where she belongs.

I'm a person who sees ghosts, and nobody will believe her.

I'm a person who's scared.

But I'm not going to fall apart.

She could almost make herself believe it.

Chapter Eleven

When she woke the next morning, the sky was the color of wet stone, and the windows were streaked with rain. Gwen went downstairs to find Dena emptying cupboards onto already crowded counters.

"It's that kind of day," Dena said dully. "We can't go outside, so I might as well get something done in here. The cupboards have needed cleaning for weeks."

"Where's Tessie?" Usually it wasn't necessary to ask. Tessie might be tiny, but she was loud.

"Gone with her father to spend a day with her best friend in Winfield. They met at our sitter's house last year, and ever since they've taken turns visiting each other. Frank will pick her up after work tonight. And Jason's working on his play,

I guess. He was supposed to clean the garage, but he can't move things outside in this weather."

"I'll help with the cupboards as soon as I have breakfast," Gwen offered. "Aunt Mary and I used to do it together every spring."

"Great." Dena's frown disappeared briefly. "It'll be nice to have company. And maybe you can keep me awake. Frank couldn't sleep last night — I think he's coming down with a cold. Between his sniffling and coughing and the thunder, I didn't rest much. How about you?" She turned away, as though reluctant to hear Gwen's reply.

"I slept all right."

"Good."

The rain was coming down harder now, beating a brisk tattoo against the kitchen window. A cupboard below the sink hung open, and taped to the inside Gwen glimpsed a picture obviously torn from a magazine. Two girls, one tiny and dark-haired, the other tall with long blonde hair, were walking away through a woods. Sunlight sifted through the trees and dappled their blue jeans and bright-colored tops.

Dena frowned as Gwen stooped for a better look.

"What are you looking at? What's in there?"

Gwen swung the door wide and pointed. "The

little girl looks sort of like Tessie," she commented. "Don't you think so?"

Dena flushed, then reached down and ripped the picture from the door. "I didn't know she taped that there!" she exclaimed. "She showed it to me — I guess she thought it looked like her, too. But it doesn't. Not really." She crumpled the picture into a ball and tossed it into the wastebasket. Then she turned back to the table and reached for a stack of hand-painted plates. "These are old and fragile," she said, changing the subject firmly. "I wouldn't trust them to the dishwasher."

Gwen ate her breakfast and set to work. Gradually the frown lines faded from Dena's forehead as they fitted new, bright-colored paper on the shelves and returned the freshly washed plates to their places. But she was quieter than usual, and it was clear that the picture on the cupboard door had disturbed her. I know she doesn't care if Tessie tacks up a picture she wants to save, Gwen thought. Dena does it herself all the time. So it must be the picture itself that upsets her — a little girl walking with an older girl who has long blonde hair. . . .

An hour sped by, then another, and the counters were nearly cleared. Dena straightened and stretched. "Snacktime," she murmured. "You fix a plate of cookies, and I'll pour some milk. Let's go into the living room and relax."

"Okay." Gwen shifted a last stack of plates into a cupboard and then took one of them out again for the cookies. She followed Dena down the hall, shivering a little as they left the brightly lit kitchen behind them. The big house, so cheerful and inviting on a sunny day, was dreary in the rain.

"What weather!" Dena set the glasses on an end table next to the couch and reached toward a lamp. As she did so, a tiny movement on the other side of the room caught Gwen's eye.

"Dena, look!" She pointed at the rocking chair close to the bay window. The ghost-girl was sitting there, one white hand on the arm of the chair, the other in her lap. When Gwen spoke, she turned slightly, and their eyes met in a long look. The cookie plate tilted, spilling its contents to the floor.

"What is it?" Dena looked from Gwen to the bay window. "What's wrong? Did you see a mouse?"

The rocking chair was empty.

"Mice won't hurt you." Dena sounded amused. "They're part of living in the country — though not the most pleasant part, I'll admit. I'll set a couple of traps tonight."

Gwen was rigid with shock. "N-not a mouse,"

she stammered. "It was that girl — the one I told you about. She was sitting right there, looking out the window."

Dena's face lost its color. "Not again, Gwen," she groaned. "Don't say things like that. I was right here, and I didn't see a thing."

"But *I* did!" Suddenly Gwen was shouting. "I saw the girl sitting there, and I saw her go into the basement night before last, and I saw her in Tessie's bedroom window the day I came here. Why won't you believe me?"

Dena sank down on the couch. "I *can't* believe you," she said shakily. "If I believed you, I'd — " She stared at her hands clenched in her lap.

"You'd what?" Gwen forced herself to speak more quietly. "You start to tell me what's wrong, and then you stop."

"I don't know what you mean," Dena protested. "Nothing's wrong. I'm sure you think you've seen a ghost, but, honestly, Gwen, there is no such thing." She tried to smile, but the corners of her mouth quivered. "What would your aunt say if she heard you? I bet she didn't believe in ghosts."

Gwen knelt and began to pick up the scattered cookies, her eyes swimming with tears. It wasn't fair to mention Aunt Mary. Life in the little house on Barker Drive had been uncomplicated — no ghosts, and no arguments, either. She had taken those peaceful days for granted, and with all her heart she longed to have them back.

"I'm sorry, dear." Dena slid off the couch and put an arm around Gwen's shoulders. "I shouldn't have mentioned your aunt. And I wasn't laughing at you. I just don't want you to get in a state over nothing."

"It isn't *nothing*," Gwen said. She stood up and set the cookie plate on the end table. "I'm not hungry. I'm going upstairs for a while."

"If you want to." Dena sounded relieved. "We're both tired, and this weather doesn't help. A little sunshine, and everything will be all right."

No, it won't, Gwen thought furiously. We're not arguing because we're tired or because it's raining. We're arguing because I'm telling the truth, and you don't want to hear it.

She felt frustrated and helpless as she climbed the front stairs and hurried down the hall to her room. The ghost-girl was becoming more daring, showing herself in the daylight and close by, but Dena would never admit Mercy Manor was haunted, even if she saw the girl herself. I think she's as frightened as I am, Gwen fumed. So why won't she talk about it?

Overhead, the attic floor creaked. Jason must

be up there, working on whatever it was. Gwen envied him. She wished she had something of her very own to think about, something so important that nothing else mattered.

She opened a window and discovered the rain had turned to mist. Out of sight, just beyond the trees, a car scrunched along the gravel road. Then it turned into the yard. The kitchen door slammed as Frank climbed out of the driver's seat. Dena hurried across the wet grass to greet him.

Scraps of their conversation drifted up to Gwen's window. " . . . sore throat — feel hot . . . pick up Tessie later." Frank turned his face up to the cooling mist, and Gwen ducked backward, not wanting to be caught eavesdropping. " . . . thought I'd better come home and rest for a while."

She peered around the curtain and watched the Mercys walk toward the house, arm in arm. Dena's head was bowed, and she was talking about something that clearly worried her more than her husband's cold. Twice before they climbed the porch steps and came into the house, Gwen heard her own name mentioned.

She's probably telling him how weird I am! Gwen hesitated for only a moment, then tiptoed across the bedroom and out into the hall. Downstairs in the kitchen the conversation continued.

Dena was still doing most of the talking, and the few words Gwen was able to hear made her hold her breath.

" . . . have to move." Dena sounded as if she were crying. "How can we stay here with this going on?"

There was an explosive sneeze that seemed to blow away Frank's patience.

"Nothing's going on!" he exclaimed loudly. "Gwen has an overactive imagination, and I'm beginning to think you do, too. You love this house, for pete's sake. How can you talk about moving?"

"But what if it's true? What if — "

Frank sneezed again. "Craziness! If Gwen's going to upset you like this, she shouldn't be living here. I thought you liked having her!"

"I do! Keep your voice down, Frank — she'll hear you! Anyway, maybe she won't mention it again. I told her she had to forget it."

There was a moment of exasperated silence, then heavy footsteps started up the back stairs. "I'm going to bed." Frank sneezed again. "We'll talk later."

Gwen darted into her room, her mind a jumble of confusion and pain. She had been right about Dena being afraid to hear the truth, but it was Frank's words that disturbed her most. If Gwen's going to upset you like this, she shouldn't be living here. She had thought he was her friend.

The footsteps stopped at the top of the stairs. She heard Frank mumble something under his breath, and then the attic door was jerked open.

"Who's up there?" Frank roared. "Is that you, Jason?"

"I'm coming down." Jason's voice cracked with tension, but his father was already on his way up the steps, sneezing furiously as he climbed.

Gwen sat down on the edge of her bed. Overhead, footsteps thumped across the attic floor, and she could hear Frank's heavy tones and his son's brief replies. What could Jason be doing up there? she wondered. For a moment her own unhappiness was forgotten as she pictured the confrontation between the Mercy men. With Frank already sick and irritable, this was the worst possible time for him to discover Jason's mysterious project.

They were coming downstairs. Gwen wished she'd closed her bedroom door, but when Frank and Jason stepped out into the hall, they were too involved with each other to realize she was watching and listening.

"Sure it's clever, but it's a complete waste of time," Frank snapped. "Can't anybody else in that school figure out how to make the thing work?"

"That's not why I did it," Jason said. "You don't understand."

"You bet I don't!" Frank coughed and blew his nose. "I don't understand why you're so — so — "

"Different." Jason's voice cracked on the word and then steadied. Gwen saw him straighten his shoulders and look at his father squarely. "You want a jock for a son, but that's not me. Why don't you give me a chance?"

They stared at each other for a moment, then Frank turned away and Jason followed him down the hall. Gwen tiptoed across the braided rug to close the door.

Jason had answered his father pretty well, she thought. He had sounded sure of himself and what he was doing. She wondered if Frank had noticed. It was hard to make grown-ups hear you if they didn't want to believe.

Chapter Twelve

She stepped down from the bus and looked around anxiously. In front of her was a small building — a bus station or a country store — and beyond the building, fields of grain stretched in every direction. Other people were getting off the bus, too, girls she knew from school, all laughing and calling to each other. One by one they were gathered up by their families and disappeared around the side of the building. No one spoke to her, or even looked at her. No one came to meet her. . . .

Gwen woke up and stared into the darkness, trying to put the dream out of her mind. It was hard to do. The endless fields still stretched behind her eyes, and she seemed to hear the murmur of voices as her friends walked away from her with the people who had come to take them home.

Gradually she realized that the sounds she heard were not just an echo from her dream. A man was speaking in a harsh whisper, and Gwen woke fully as she became aware that the voice was coming from the backyard. Burglars! Who else would be prowling around the yard in the middle of the night? She slipped out of bed and hurried to the window.

The rain had stopped, and the moon was blurred behind low clouds. The backyard looked unfamiliar, even sinister, in the faint light. At first it seemed empty, though the whispering continued. She heard the word "accident," and then, "Get this over with." There was a hollow quality in the voice, as though the whisperer were speaking from the depths of a cave.

Gwen wondered if she should run down the hall and wake Frank. He would want to know if someone were breaking in, wouldn't he? Then she remembered his irritability that afternoon and his suggestion that she might have to leave Mercy Manor if she couldn't control her imagination. If she woke him and there was no sign of the whisperer, he would be more annoyed than ever.

She moved the curtains to one side, and as she did so the clouds drifted from the face of the moon and the yard was flooded with light. Two figures sprang into view at the foot of the porch steps.

One of them carried a heavy bundle; his shoulders were hunched, and as he moved across the lawn he shifted the weight in his arms. They must have already been in the house, Gwen thought with dismay. She wondered what they had stolen. If the Mercys had expensive silver, it was still packed away in the basement. The television set? The weight the man carried was too long and narrow to be a television set.

As if in answer to her unspoken question, the figure shifted the bundle again and flung it over his shoulder. Long blonde hair cascaded down his back, and a slim white arm dangled loosely. Gwen gasped and stumbled backward as the two figures turned their faces toward her window. An instant later they had vanished, but not before she recognized them. She had seen them before, a young man and a middle-aged one, struggling with a boat at the riverbank and posed in the photograph she'd found in the basement.

With a little moan of terror Gwen sank down on the braided rug. I didn't see them! I didn't! If she said it often enough, maybe she could make the nightmare vision go away. Two men stealing across the lawn, carrying someone with long blonde hair. . . . Two men who couldn't possibly be here . . . now . . . in the Mercys' backyard. . . .

The darkness was suffocating. Gwen scrambled across the room on her knees and switched on the bedside lamp. Then she stood up on trembling legs and went back to close the window, careful not to look outside. Sleep was impossible, but she climbed into bed anyway and pulled the sheet up to her chin. She hoped Dena wouldn't get up and notice the light; she tried turning off the lamp, but panic swept over her and she quickly turned it on again.

The hours that followed were the longest of Gwen's life. When the windows finally turned gray with morning light, she got up and dressed hurriedly, eager to put the night behind her.

She was about to tiptoe down the back stairs when Tessie's door opened and the little girl came into the hall, looking like an elf in her green pajamas.

"Where're you going, Gwennie?"

"Just downstairs," Gwen whispered. "I don't feel like sleeping."

"I'll come with you. I don't feel like sleeping either."

"How about your slippers?"

"Don't need 'em. I like bare feet." Tessie led the way down to the kitchen and then on to the back door. "We can go outside," she said hopefully. "Sometimes there's bunnies early in the morning."

They went out on the porch and looked across the glittering, rain-soaked lawn. They were right there, Gwen thought with a shudder. The men had walked from the porch steps across the grass toward the woods with their dreadful burden. It seemed impossible in the daylight, just as it seemed impossible that she had seen the ghost-girl sitting in the living room yesterday afternoon.

If I can hardly believe it myself, she thought, how can I ever convince anyone else that this is really happening?

"If you're very quiet, the bunnies will come," Tessie said in a not very quiet voice.

She sat on the top step, and Gwen joined her, grateful for the little girl's company. Five minutes passed, a long time for Tessie to be still. Then there were sounds in the kitchen behind them, and Jason came out on the porch eating a banana. He looked startled when he saw them sitting there.

"Didn't know anyone else was up."

"We're looking for bunnies," Tessie explained. "I think there was one just going to come out, but you scared him away."

Jason sat down next to her. "Couldn't sleep," he said briefly.

Remembering Frank's anger, Gwen thought she understood. Still, Jason seemed different today, more relaxed and at peace with himself. Perhaps he was relieved that he no longer had any secrets from his father.

"Daddy's cross," Tessie said, her eyes still on the bushes where a rabbit might, or might not, appear. "He doesn't want you to go up in the attic."

Jason ruffled her cap of dark hair. "I know that."

"He told Mama that thing you're making is a waste of time."

"I know that, too. It's *his* opinion."

"Can Gwennie and I go up in the attic and see it?"

Gwen held her breath, expecting a flat refusal, but to her amazement Jason just shrugged. "If you want to. And if you promise not to touch."

"I promise." Tessie jumped to her feet, the bunnies forgotten. "Let's go now," she begged, taking Gwen's hand.

Gwen looked at Jason. She was as curious as Tessie was, but his willingness confused her. "Do you want me to go, too?" she asked cautiously.

"Why not?"

They trooped indoors with Tessie leading the way. In the kitchen, Jason and Gwen took off their shoes so they wouldn't be heard. Then they all tiptoed up the back stairs and on to the attic.

Thin, early morning light streamed through small windows at either end of the big room. It touched a cluster of suitcases, a rack of clothes in plastic bags, and a few boxes pushed back along the walls. Otherwise the attic was empty except for a huge carton in the middle of the floor. The carton was upside-down, its flaps splayed out. Tessie ran to it and bent to lift one of the flaps.

"Don't touch — you promised." Jason pulled a cord to turn on the dangling lightbulb, then crouched and lifted the carton by himself.

Gwen stared in astonishment. A miniature stage, perfect in every detail, stood before them. Blue velvet curtains were looped back on either side, and a tiny blue and gold emblem decorated the middle of the crosspiece overhead.

"That's the stage in the high school auditorium!" she exclaimed. "I've been there for plays lots of times."

Jason looked pleased. "Now watch this," he said. He reached around to the back of the stage, and suddenly a row of tiny footlights flashed on. Tessie squealed with delight.

"But why did you build it?" Gwen wanted to

know. "What's it for? It must have taken hours and hours."

"It did," Jason admitted. "That's why my dad is so mad — I told you he would be. But I had to do it to prove something. See, the Drama Club usually picks plays that need a single set — that makes the play easier to produce. Most of my play takes place in a classroom, but there's one scene in the second act that has to be in the teachers' lounge. I tried to figure out how to change that, but I couldn't do it. So I invented a way to change the set easily — fast, too. Kneel down and I'll show you."

Gwen dropped to her knees in front of the stage and examined the miniature classroom. Five tiny two-person desks and ten chairs were arranged in front of the teacher's desk. The walls were covered with skillfully painted chalkboards, and there was a bookshelf and a cupboard in the back of the room. Bright-colored little books of folded cardboard were scattered on the desktops, and there was a tiny apple on the teacher's desk.

"What's the apple for?" Tessie demanded. "Did you make it?"

"The apple's a joke," Jason explained patiently. "And, yes, I made it — I stole some of your modeling clay."

Tessie looked at him with suspicion. "I don't have any red."

"I stole some of Mom's nail polish, too." He was studying Gwen's expression. "What do *you* think?"

"I think it's just — wonderful!" She leaned forward for a better look at the two-inch-high portrait of Abraham Lincoln hanging behind the teacher's desk. "I didn't know you were a writer *and* an artist."

Jason hid his pleasure with another demonstration. "I told you I built the stage to prove a change of scene would be simple. Here's how it works." He moved the desks, the chairs, and the teacher's desk to the sides of the stage. Then he reached back and pulled one section of the chalkboard forward, turning it smoothly with his index finger. A low, narrow platform, attached to the back of the chalkboard, swung into view. On it stood a couch, a chair, and a low table. The walls were covered with posters and "announcements," and there were magazines scattered on the table.

"Now all you have to do is pull the curtains halfway to hide the classroom stuff" — he loosened the gold cords that held the curtains back — "and there it is, the teachers' lounge! Pretty neat, huh?"

"Oh, yes!" Gwen forgot that Jason had

laughed at her problem, that she wasn't even sure she liked him. "It's the neatest thing I've ever seen. If I was your teacher, I'd tell the Drama Club they have to put on your play. I'd *make* them do it."

Jason grinned. "You haven't even read it. Maybe you'd think it was awful."

"No, I wouldn't," Gwen said earnestly. "I mean, you'd know if it was awful, and you'd keep working till you fixed it." Once again she felt a pang of envy. He knew exactly what he wanted, and he was going to make it happen. He'd even managed to stand up to his father.

All I do is feel sorry for myself, she thought.

"What's the matter?" Jason asked. "You look funny."

Before she could answer, Tessie scrambled to her feet. "Mama's awake," she said. "I hear her downstairs. Can I tell her about the little school?"

"She knows all about it," Jason replied. "I showed it to her a couple of days ago." He turned off the footlights and pushed the chalkboard back into place. "She thought it was great," he told Gwen. "But she knew it would make Dad blow up. And she was right — he hated it. But at least we had it out. And I didn't act like a wimp."

Gwen stood up. She thought of her brother opening her last letter with a groan, or — more painful yet — putting it aside, wishing he didn't have to open it at all. More complaints, more whining — that's what he'd expect. And he'd be right. Her face burned at the thought. She wished she could handle her problems alone, the way Jason handled his.

"Going out on the porch again?" he asked, but Gwen shook her head. She wanted to be by herself for a while.

Back in her bedroom, she stood at the window and stared down at the spot where she'd seen the ghosts last night. If she was going to solve her own problems, the ghosts of Mercy Manor were where she had to start. They were showing themselves to her and to no one else. She could go on panicking because there was no one to help her, or she could gather her courage and use her wits to find out why the ghosts were there.

Chapter Thirteen

"Do you like brown horses or black horses?" Tessie tapped Gwen's bare knee with a crayon.

"Green," Gwen said lazily. "I'd like a green horse." She was curled up with a book at one end of the porch swing, and Tessie was at the other, bent over her coloring book.

"That's silly," Tessie said. "There aren't any green horses."

"It's a nice color, though." Gwen waved a hand at the expanse of lawn and the wall of fluttering leaves where the woods began. "I wouldn't *mind* a green horse, would you?"

Tessie looked pained. "Brown's better," she said and bent over her book.

Gwen leaned back and stretched. It had been a quiet day, and she had slept soundly last night, with no interruptions. Perhaps that was why she felt so relaxed. Or perhaps it was because her fear of the ghosts of Mercy Manor was not quite so intense now that she had made up her mind to solve the mystery behind their coming. Not that I want to see them again, she admitted to herself. But if they do come back, next time I'm going to be ready.

"Telephone, Gwen." Dena spoke through the screen, smiling at the girls in their cozy nest of cushions. "I think it's one of your friends from school."

Gwen jumped up and hurried into the house. She hoped the caller wasn't Sandy Barber. She still felt uncomfortable every time she remembered their meeting in the mall.

"Gwen? It's Julie."

"Julie!" Gwen turned just in time to see Jason pass the doorway. He grinned as her voice shot up in a squeal of delight.

"I'm home — just an hour ago. How are you? Can you come to town Saturday and stay overnight?" The words tumbled out without a break. "My mom wants me to help her with the laundry and cleaning and stuff the rest of this week."

Saturday was two whole days away, but it didn't matter. Julie was back in Winfield!

"That'll be fine," Gwen said eagerly. "I'll get Jason to bring me."

"Who's Jason?"

"He's my — my foster brother." The words sounded awkward. She hurried on, in case Jason was still listening. "I've got lots to tell you. Did you have a good time in Oregon?"

"Great, except that my brothers were pests all the way out there and all the way back. You're lucky to have a brother old enough to drive. Mine aren't good for anything."

"Julie, shame on you!" Gwen heard Julie's mother in the background, and she giggled. Saturday! she thought. Oh, Saturday! It was going to be hard to wait.

Later, when she wandered into the living room, Dena and Jason smiled at her. "You look — shining," Dena told her. "Was that your friend who's been away on vacation?"

"Julie." Gwen nodded happily. "She wants me to sleep over at her house Saturday. Is that okay?"

"Of course. She'll have to come out here to stay with you sometime, too. You can invite anyone you want, you know. We can put up a cot in your room."

"That'll be fun," Gwen said politely. But she

heard the hesitation in her own voice, as she pictured Julie walking around a corner and confronting the ghost-girl. Or looking out the window at night and seeing . . . Resolutely, she turned away from those thoughts. Once she solved the mystery of the ghosts, everything would change.

"I'll take you to town on Saturday," Jason offered. "I want to pick up a couple more props for my stage set."

He said it casually, but Gwen could tell he liked talking openly about his work. She glanced over her shoulder, half-expecting to see Frank scowling in the doorway. Then she remembered that he'd gone back to work today, still sneezing.

When she returned to the porch, Tessie was busy with a new page in her coloring book. "What color should I make the rooster?" she wondered.

"Pink and purple," Gwen suggested. "Or blue and green — that would be neat." She threw herself down on the swing to think about Saturday.

"How about black and silver?" Jason suggested, following her out and sitting down between them. "A sort of metal robot-rooster."

"You're making all that up," Tessie said scornfully. "Red and yellow are better."

"Tessie takes after my dad," Jason said. "She doesn't like craziness, do you, kid?"

But neither do you, thought Gwen. Seeing ghosts is a kind of craziness, and you certainly didn't want to hear about that! Still, she wasn't nearly as angry with him as she had been before. They had a lot in common, even if he didn't realize it.

"You know what?" Jason demanded suddenly. "Just now, in the living room, that was the first time I ever saw you looking happy. Really happy, I mean."

Gwen turned to him in surprise. "Well, I haven't heard *you* do much but gripe and grumble since I got here," she retorted. Then she relented. "But I guess you have a lot on your mind. I'd like to read your play some time — if you want me to."

"Okay."

They sat companionably, looking out over the yard at a pair of robins arguing about a juicy worm. Gwen wished she could make this moment last.

"Red and yellow are best," Tessie said smugly. "I told you so." She held up the book so they could see.

That night Gwen went to bed wearing jeans and a T-shirt, her sneakers close by where she could slide into them quickly. Next to them she placed the flashlight she'd smuggled from the kitchen drawer. Her heart pounded as if she were already seeing eerie figures moving across the grass. She had made up her mind that, if the men came back, she would follow them to the very edge of the woods. But only that far! She would try to see where they were going, but she couldn't possibly go in after them. And she would have to be ready to move quickly if she was going to do even that much.

When her digital clock said midnight, she slipped out of bed and crouched in front of the window. Moonlight silvered the lawn; she could hardly make out the bulk of the barn in the darkness. Insects sang, and something small and roly-poly waddled across the grass between the deepest shadows.

When the first sound came, it was so close that Gwen rocked back on her heels in fright. Tessie's door had opened. Maybe she was going to the bathroom, Gwen thought, but the steps that sounded in the hall were not Tessie's. And they were going toward the back stairs.

Gwen stepped into her sneakers and snatched up the flashlight. She hurried out into the hall.

Tessie's door was open a couple of inches. She pushed it far enough to peek in and make sure the little girl was still snuggled in bed. Then, flashlight in hand, Gwen started down the stairs. The pencil of light cut through total darkness until she reached the back hall. There, a pale glow from the open basement door told her what she was going to have to do next.

Reluctantly, she peered into the basement. The figure of the ghost-girl hovered halfway down the stairs in its cocoon of shimmering light. As Gwen hesitated, not sure she could make herself follow, the girl turned and looked back, then raised one hand in a pleading gesture.

I've got to go with her. Gwen tried desperately to call up the determination she had felt a few minutes before. Trembling, she took one step, then another, down into the basement she'd never wanted to visit again.

When she reached the bottom, the ghost was already halfway across the big, dark room. Gwen's stomach lurched as she saw a strip of light under the door leading to the fruit cellar. There was a murmur of voices from the other side. She recognized one of them; it was the same harsh whisper she'd heard in the yard two nights ago.

Don't go in! She wanted to shout a warning to the girl who was moving more slowly now, with frequent glances backward. Sick at heart, Gwen realized she couldn't change whatever was about to happen. This was why the ghost-girl had wanted her to follow. This was what she was supposed to see.

"WHO'S DOWN THERE?"

Light flared behind her, freezing Gwen where she stood. The scream that rose in her throat was choked off as footsteps thundered down the basement steps. She turned to face Frank Mercy, a truly terrifying figure with his arm raised over his head, clutching a flashlight like a club.

Chapter Fourteen

"What is it, Frank? What's happening?"

Dena was at the top of the stairs with Jason beside her, framed by light from the kitchen. She was so pale that Gwen hardly recognized her.

"Gwen, what are you doing down here?" Frank demanded. "What's going on?"

They can see for themselves now! Gwen turned to point at the ghost-girl, but the basement was dark. The shimmering light had vanished. Her flashlight picked out the dark fruit cellar door.

"She was right here — the ghost! And someone was in the fruit cellar!" Gwen struggled to convince them, but the words sounded foolish in her own ears. There was no one else in the basement.

"You're out of your mind," Frank said harshly.

"I mean it! If you have to pull a dumb stunt like this to get attention — "

"She *was* here!" Gwen repeated desperately. "It was the girl I told Dena about. And she was going toward the fruit cellar when you shouted. A light was on in there, and people were talking. You have to believe me!" Now that she'd started, she wanted to tell him about the figures in the yard, too, but the look on his face stopped her.

"Somebody's been talking all right," he said angrily, "and I don't mean ghosts in the fruit cellar! You've been scaring Dena out of her wits with your stories. Now go on upstairs."

Gwen edged past him and made her way up the steps. At the top Jason and Dena moved back and followed her into the kitchen.

"Oh, Gwen you shouldn't have," Dena whispered. "I told you to forget all this — just don't think about it. Now Frank is angry. . . ."

She was right about that. Frank seemed to fill the kitchen as he faced Gwen across the table. How could I ever have thought he liked me? she wondered. He looks like he might blow up! As if in answer to the thought, Frank sneezed mightily and snatched a paper napkin from the rack in the middle of the table. If he catches pneumonia, that'll be my fault, too. He's going to tell me to pack up and go.

"Let's not talk now," Dena begged. "You don't feel well, Frank, and we're all tired."

Frank looked at her white face. "Okay," he said gruffly, "but we've got to straighten this out tomorrow." He scowled at Gwen. "Everybody back to bed now — and this time, stay there!" He took Dena's arm and started toward the back stairs, sneezing all the way.

When they had gone, Jason shook his head in disbelief. "Still seeing ghosts, huh?" he said. His tone was light, but he eyed Gwen intently.

"It's not funny," she said. "You don't know what it's like, having people say you're crazy."

"Sure, I do. I'm the nut who'd rather play with a stage in the attic than join the basketball team, remember?"

Gwen smiled weakly. "Okay, you do know," she agreed. "But they're not going to send you away because you don't play basketball."

"What are you talking about?"

"I heard your dad and mother talking yesterday. I *eavesdropped*," she added, before he could accuse her. "Your dad said I was upsetting your mom, and if I kept on doing it I'd have to move out. And your mom said you might all have to move. He's right; I do upset her when I talk about ghosts. It's as if I'm forcing her to think about things she doesn't want to think about. But it's

not my fault!" She looked across the hall at the
door to the back stairs, half-expecting to see the
ghost-girl hovering there. "I can't pretend not to
see, can I?"

"Jason. Gwen." Dena's whisper floated down
the stairwell. "Will you please turn out the lights
and come up to bed?"

They stared at each other. Then Jason reached
for the light switch, and Gwen turned on the
flashlight she was clutching.

"What do you mean, you force her to think
about things she doesn't want to think about?"
Jason asked in a low voice. "My mother doesn't
have any deep, dark secrets."

"I don't know what I mean." That was the
trouble, Gwen thought, as she turned in to her
bedroom and closed the door behind her. How
could you try to solve a mystery if you didn't
know what the real mystery was?

She climbed into bed and thought about what
had happened in these last frightening minutes.
The ghost-girl wanted me to follow her down to
the basement — I'm sure of that. And I'm sure
there was someone — or something — in the
fruit cellar tonight, no matter what Frank says.
But I still don't know who the girl is or why she
wants me to follow her, and I don't know why
Dena doesn't like to hear about her.

She was no closer to finding answers to her questions than she had been before, and now Frank was furious with her. All that determination to solve the mystery by herself had just made things worse.

She woke early, but the sound of Frank's deep voice down in the kitchen kept her in her room. She didn't want to face him any sooner than she had to. Maybe if she could talk to him quietly, she thought, without Dena standing by looking terrified. . . .

The back door opened and closed, and from her window she watched Frank stride across the yard to the car and stand there a moment before getting in. He's feeling better, she thought, and her spirits lifted a bit. If Frank was beginning to recover from his cold, he might be more forgiving about what had happened last night. But then she saw his shoulders slump tiredly, and when he climbed into the car, his expression was grim.

Jason was still at the table, nibbling toast and reading when she went downstairs. Before he could speak, Tessie dashed in from the dining room to make elaborate shushing noises.

"Mama's resting," she said importantly. "She has a bad headache."

Because of last night! Gwen thought, more depressed than ever.

"If your mom is trying to sleep, you'd better take your shoes off," she warned Tessie. "You sound like a whole herd of elephants."

Tessie looked at her in surprise but sat down on the floor to do as she was told.

"*Little* elephants," Gwen added, by way of an apology. "I guess I'm kind of grumpy today."

"You and everybody else," Jason said. "My dad was so mad at the world he forgot to give me my work orders. Lucky for him I was going to clean the garage today anyway. The sooner I get that out of the way, the better I'll like it." He looked at Tessie, who was admiring her bare pink toes. "How about picking some flowers for Mom," he suggested. "Surprise her."

Tessie didn't move. "From the field or from the garden?"

He pretended to think. "From the garden," he said. "This once. But not too many," he called as she started toward the door.

When she was out of earshot, he looked at Gwen thoughtfully. "You don't really think my folks are going to kick you out, do you?" he asked. "They aren't like that."

"They won't want to do it," Gwen replied, "but they'll think they have to — especially if I decide to tell them what I saw in the backyard a couple of nights ago. They'd flip if they heard that."

"In the backyard?" Jason repeated. "Come on!"

Gwen stiffened. "Just forget it," she snapped. "I don't need you laughing at me."

"Who's laughing?" he protested. "Tell me what you saw."

Gwen looked at him with suspicion. Then she pulled out a chair and sat down. "I wasn't going to mention the ghosts again to anybody," she said resignedly. "I wanted to figure out what was happening all by myself. But then last night, your dad heard me — "

"The backyard," Jason prompted. "What did you see?"

Haltingly, Gwen told him. "The men were Dena's uncle and cousin. At least, I think that's who they were. I recognized them from a photograph. And they were carrying a body, Jason! I saw them! It was horrible!"

Jason propped his chin on his hand and stared at her wonderingly. "You know, you're the one who should be the writer, and I — I'll play basketball and make my dad's day." He grinned teasingly, but Gwen didn't smile back.

"See? I knew you wouldn't believe me," she snapped. "It's no use talking to you! But I have a theory about what's happening here, and I think I'm right."

Jason wiped away the smile with the back of his hand. "So what's the big theory?"

"That body those men were carrying was the ghost-girl. They killed her for some reason — I haven't figured that out yet — and I think their spirits are going to keep acting out the crime again and again until the truth is uncovered. Of course the men don't really *want* people to know what they did, but they haven't any choice — that's what I believe. And the ghost-girl *does* want us to know what happened. That's why she keeps trying to make me follow her."

"Where in the world did you get all *that*?" Jason demanded. "How do you know what ghosts want?"

"It's like you said a few days ago," Gwen told him coolly. "I've read lots of ghost stories — made-up ones and true ones, too, about ghosts that haunt houses right here in the Midwest. Ghosts *want* to rest in peace, but they can't when something is troubling them. I think a terrible crime was committed here a long time ago, and everyone who was part of what happened then is going to go on haunting Mercy Manor until someone figures out the truth. That's what I think" — she glared at him — "but who's going to believe me?"

"Nobody," Jason said at once. He leaned forward, his long face earnest. "Look, I don't know what's going on — if anything — but that's my mother's relatives you're calling murderers. My folks could never take a story like that seriously — not in a million years. And that's why you don't have to worry!" he finished triumphantly. "My mom's upset because she wants to be a good foster mother, and she doesn't know what to do with a kid who thinks she sees ghosts. And my dad just wants my mother to be happy. So if you stay in your room at night, and quit talking about ghosts during the day — "

Gwen pushed back her chair and stood up. "I knew I shouldn't tell anyone," she said bitterly. "Especially you. You don't care about other people's problems — just your own!"

Jason looked indignant. "That's not true. I'm just telling you that if you keep still, you'll stay out of trouble with my folks. I do it all the time — keep my mouth shut, I mean."

"Not all the time," Gwen corrected him. "I heard you and Frank talking after he saw your theater. You didn't keep still then. And you didn't keep still at the dinner table the other night."

Jason flushed. "That was different." He hesitated, then grinned unexpectedly. "Well, I guess speaking up made me feel better, but it didn't change his mind, did it? So the advice still stands."

"Thanks a lot!" Gwen didn't know what else to say. He didn't believe her, and yet she could tell that this time he had really wanted to help. The trouble with his so-called advice was that it left her squarely where she had been before. Frightened and alone.

Chapter Fifteen

Frank Mercy was waiting on the porch when Gwen and Tessie returned that afternoon from a walk along the edge of the woods, all the way to the sunflower field. For a little while, Gwen had lost herself in the gold and green beauty of the day, but the moment she saw Frank, all her worries came rushing back. He was home earlier than usual. His expression was grim. He looks the way I feel when I go to the dentist, she thought with a sinking heart. Just wanting to get it over with.

"We saw three bunnies," Tessie reported. "And a long, dark thing that ran into the woods."

"It might have been a mink," Gwen offered. "I've never seen one before."

Frank didn't seem to hear. "Tessie, go tell Mama you're back," he ordered. "She's feeling a little better, but she's still lying down." He gestured impatiently. "Go ahead now. Maybe you can get her a cold cloth for her head, or something."

Tessie hesitated, aware that she was being sent away for a reason. Then, unable to resist playing nurse, she opened the screen door and darted inside.

Frank motioned toward the swing. "You've been awfully good with Tessie, Gwen," he said gruffly. "We appreciate that."

Gwen sat down. She wished she could cover her ears to shut out what Frank was going to say next.

"But we have a problem here, and I guess you know what it is. This stuff you've been carrying on about" — he held up a hand to keep Gwen from interrupting — "it's very hard on Dena. She's been kind of low anyway, off and on, and I hoped that having you here would cheer her up. It hasn't worked that way. The more you insist on this crazy ghost business, the worse she feels. Today she's been flat on her back in bed — miserable!" Frank's voice rose. "We can't have that! I think the best thing to do is to make a change — the sooner, the better. Better for you, too."

"You want me to move," Gwen said flatly. It

was easier to speak the words herself than to hear him say them.

Frank rubbed a big hand over his face. "That's the way it is. Dena can't stand any extra stress, so before you get too settled in . . . I've told her I'm going to call the Social Services office. I'll talk to your brother first, of course. Between us, I'm sure we can figure out something. You'll be happier in another place."

No, I won't! Gwen wanted to shout it at him. She stared out at the lawn, the flowerbeds, the woods on one side and the meadow on the other, then back at Frank's unhappy face. He had tried to be a father to her, and Dena had welcomed her like a mother. If it hadn't been for the ghosts, forcing themselves into her life, spoiling everything, Mercy Manor would be her permanent home, and this would have been the family Aunt Mary had wished for her. She knew that now, when it was too late.

"It would help if you'd go upstairs and tell Dena the move is okay with you," Frank suggested. "She doesn't want you to leave, but she agrees that things can't go on like this. She's getting more depressed all the time, and it's your ghosts that are doing it."

Your ghosts! The words echoed in Gwen's ears as she crossed the porch. They weren't *her* ghosts.

137

If they belonged to anyone, they were Dena's, and she refused even to talk about them.

Upstairs, the door to the master bedroom stood open. Tessie sat in the middle of the queen-sized bed, a bulky album opened across her knees. She looked up when Gwen came in.

"Mama's taking a shower," she said. "She feels better now."

"Good." Gwen started to retreat, but when Tessie patted the bed beside her, she changed her mind and sat down next to the little girl. If she went back to her bedroom — hers no longer — she would cry for sure.

"What's that you're looking at?"

Tessie snuggled closer and shifted the album to Gwen's lap. "It's Mama's picture book, starting when she was a little baby." With an effort, she turned the heavy pages back to the beginning and pointed to an infant sitting on the lap of a sweet-faced woman. "That's Mama and Grandma." She turned a page. "And here's Mama with her Aunt Josie. She used to live in this house."

Aunt Josie had short-cropped hair and somber eyes. Worried looking, Gwen thought. Like Dena.

"My grandma made this book for Mama a long time ago," Tessie explained. "And then Mama added more pictures."

She swept past the next few pages to the last third of the book, which was crowded with snapshots of Tessie in her sandbox; Jason lying on the porch swing reading; Tessie in the sunflower field; Dena and Frank next to their car. Gwen lingered over each page, reading the captions out loud, putting off the moment when she was going to have to think about the latest disaster in her life.

"Let's look at the pages we missed," she suggested. "You're going too fast. A lot must have happened between the time your mama was a little girl and now." She turned back toward the middle of the album and was surprised to discover a half-empty page. Two snapshots had been removed from the book, leaving blank spaces above their labels.

Uncle Raymond with Allen. Gwen thought of the framed picture in the basement. Dena hadn't wanted it hanging on any wall in her house, and apparently she didn't want Raymond and Allen in her album either.

Then she looked at the other neatly lettered label: *Dena in the garden with Rose.*

"Turn the page," Tessie said impatiently. "This one's dumb."

Gently Gwen moved the little hands off the page and pointed to the second caption. "This was supposed to be a picture of your mama with a person called Rose," she said shakily. "Do you know who Rose is?"

Tessie looked bored. "Just somebody," she said. "Want to see a picture of Mama in a long dress with sparkles on it?"

Gwen gave up and turned to a page of high school prom shots. But she was no longer listening to Tessie's prattle. Visions of a paper rose hovered in front of her, a rose that had suddenly taken on new meaning.

The ghost-girl leaves a paper rose, she thought excitedly. And Dena used to have a friend called Rose. Maybe it doesn't mean anything at all — but maybe it does! What if the ghost-girl was Dena's friend a long time ago, and now she's leaving the flower as a clue to tell us she's back?

Tessie pointed out her mother on a crowded gym dance floor, and Gwen nodded absently. If there was a connection between the paper rose and a real person, Dena would have figured it out long ago. But for some reason she was determined not to admit it — or even think about it — so determined that she had even taken Rose's picture out of her album.

"Tessie, Gwen isn't interested in looking at a lot of old pictures." Dena stood in the doorway, her face drawn and almost as white as the terry cloth robe she hugged around her. Barefoot and without her usual lipstick, she looked like a freshly scrubbed and thoroughly unhappy little girl.

"I don't mind," Gwen said. She and Dena stared at each other, while Tessie continued to turn the pages of the album.

"Frank told me — what you decided," Gwen said finally. "It's okay. I'm sorry about your headache."

"It's practically gone now." Dena padded across the room and curled up at the foot of the bed. "I don't want you to — " She glanced at Tessie and started over. "I don't like what you and Frank just talked about. I still think we can work this out. We can — "

Tessie scrambled across the bed, leaving the album open behind her, and Dena glanced down at the half-empty page where two pictures had been removed. Her face sagged. When she turned back to Gwen, there were tears in her eyes.

"I don't like it, but I don't know what else to do," she said painfully. "I'm so mixed up, Gwen. Maybe Frank's right. I guess you'd be better off if you moved away." She sighed. "And so would we."

Chapter Sixteen

"What's the matter with everybody?" Jason was halfway through his second helping of chicken casserole before it occurred to him that something had happened while he was in town. He looked at Gwen first, and when she didn't reply, he turned from one of his parents to the other. "What's the big deal?"

Tessie rested her chin on one small fist. "Daddy says Gwen is going to live with someone else, and Mama won't talk about it, and Gwen won't talk about it, and I'm mad." She glared around the table with a defiance that faded quickly when she met her father's stern eye.

"I told you we weren't going to discuss this during dinner, young lady," Frank said. "You have a short memory."

"What do you mean, she's going to live with someone else?" Jason demanded. "What's going on?"

"Nothing is settled," Dena said nervously. "We've just been talking. . . ."

"It *is* pretty much settled," Frank interrupted. "Gwen's stay with us hasn't worked out the way we'd hoped it would, and so we've decided to make a change. She agrees that it's the best thing to do," he added, "so don't complicate the situation by arguing."

Gwen kept her eyes on her plate. It was strange, being discussed as if she weren't there.

"Is it because of that business last night?" Jason sounded as if he couldn't believe what he was hearing. "You're going to make her leave because of some stupid — "

"That's enough!" Frank roared, so loudly that Tessie dropped her fork on her plate.

Dena pushed her chair away from the table. "My headache is coming back!" she exclaimed. "I don't feel like eating — sorry." She hurried out of the dining room, giving Gwen's shoulder a squeeze as she passed.

"Now look what you've done!" Frank growled. "Just when your mother was beginning to feel a little better. You kids — "

Tessie burst into tears and raced upstairs after

143

her mother. Gwen longed to go after them, but she felt too numbed to move.

"Don't blame me," Jason protested. "All I did was ask an innocent question. I'm not the one who's telling Gwen she has to get out."

"I said that's enough!" Frank smacked the table hard. "We're not going to talk about it anymore, and we're not going to hand out blame. Is that clear, Jason? If Gwen can handle this in a mature way, there's no reason for you to raise the roof."

Now they were both looking at Gwen, waiting for her to show how mature she was. "I think," she began, "I think — " She swallowed hard. "I think I'm going to be sick." With a hand pressed over her mouth she dashed out of the room and up the stairs, making it to the bathroom just in time.

Afterward, she sat on the bathroom floor and leaned against the old-fashioned footed tub. Three people out of five, she thought wryly. It would be laughable, the way she and Dena and Tessie had leaped up and run, one after the other, if it weren't so sad.

When she went back downstairs a few minutes later, the table had been cleared, and Jason was busy at the sink.

"You okay?" He glanced at her uneasily, obviously fearful of saying the wrong thing.

She nodded.

"Just answer one question then," he said. "Is all this happening because you keep seeing ghosts and my folks don't believe you? Are they really that upset about it?"

Gwen picked up a stack of plates and carried them to the dishwasher. "You heard your dad," she said. "He's upset, all right. And your mother is, too, but she won't admit it. I'm the reason she has the headache."

"But I told you not to keep talking about ghosts," Jason sounded exasperated. "I told you."

"It was too late — your dad had already made up his mind I should go. And besides," Gwen tried to ignore her churning stomach, "I can't pretend I've been telling lies when I haven't. There *is* something weird going on, and it's not my fault I'm the only one who believes it. I've tried to tell you." She looked at him accusingly. "All of you."

She expected another argument, but Jason stood very still and stared out the window into the twilight. "So maybe we have to move to Plan B," he said slowly. "It'll be a waste of time, but still . . . If it doesn't work, you have to promise to forget about spooks and ghoulies."

Gwen frowned. "You still think this is a joke."

"It doesn't matter what I think. I just can't believe that my folks are ready to send you away. And that you're stubborn enough to leave rather than admit you're wrong."

"I'm not wrong." Gwen was defiant. "So what's Plan B?"

"Well, I was just thinking, maybe I could stay up and watch with you for a couple of nights. It would be a sort of test."

Gwen took a deep breath. "Would you do that?"

"For a couple of nights I can stand it, I guess." Jason went back to scrubbing pans. "But you have to promise that if we don't see anything, that'll be the end of it. You'll tell my dad you were mistaken and you aren't ever going to mention ghosts again."

"But I'm not mistaken!"

He grimaced. "Then just promise you won't talk about it again. They'll go for it. My dad doesn't want you to leave any more than my mom does — I can tell. And Tessie looks as if she's lost her best teddy bear. Do you want to make them all feel terrible just because you won't give a little?"

"I love your family," Gwen said, struggling to

keep her voice steady. "If it weren't for — for the ghosts — I'd love living here."

"So what do you say?"

"They don't appear every single night."

"I said I'd watch for *two* nights, remember?"

Gwen felt relieved and trapped at the same time. "It probably won't make any difference what I promise," she said mournfully. "Frank has made up his mind."

"Wait and see," Jason told her. "Don't give up so fast."

He was really okay when you got to know him, Gwen thought — one more reason to be sorry she must leave Mercy Manor.

They finished filling the dishwasher and dried the pots and pans, making up a plan as they worked. Gwen would stay in her bedroom and listen for the ghost-girl's step in the hall. She would sit close to the window so she could watch the backyard, too. Jason would read in the living room until Frank went up to bed, and then he'd move to the kitchen where he could see the back stairs, the basement door, and, if he went to the window, the backyard.

"If Rose comes down the stairs, you'll get a good look at her, and you'll see where she goes," Gwen said. "You'll have to believe me then."

"Rose? Who's Rose?"

Gwen explained about the picture missing from the album and reminded him of the paper rose that kept appearing and disappearing.

Jason wasn't impressed. "How do you know Rose wasn't a pet dog or a cat?" he asked. "Maybe Rose was a goat! You're jumping to conclusions, for pete's sake."

In spite of his doubts, when Gwen went up to her bedroom at ten, she felt more hopeful than she had all day. Surely if the ghost-girl had a secret to reveal, she would come tonight and let Jason see her. Or the two men would walk again across the lawn. She didn't care what Jason saw, as long as he saw enough to make him believe.

It was strange to want something so much and not want it at the same time. As soon as she'd moved the rocking chair close to the open window and had settled down to wait, the terror she'd known the night before came rushing back. Reading ghost stories was fun, but being squarely in the middle of a ghost story wasn't. Even though the evening was cool, her hands were wet with perspiration, and she began to shiver.

A little after eleven Frank came upstairs, trying to be quiet but not succeeding very well. Then the mysterious creakings of the old house took over. After so many nights of waiting and listening, Gwen knew them all. There were faint brushing sounds that might be footsteps but were not, and sudden sharp cracks that made her heart leap. She thought of Jason downstairs in the kitchen. Did his arms and legs ache with tension, the way hers did? She doubted it. After all, he was there to prove to Gwen that she was wrong. He didn't expect to see anything at all.

An hour passed. Gwen tiptoed across the room and took down a blanket from the closet shelf. The cozy warmth felt good around her shoulders, reminding her of nights in the little house on Barker Drive when she had sat up in bed reading for hours. Keep thinking about that, she told herself, but Barker Drive seemed a long time ago, another life.

Her sight began to blur from staring into the moonlit backyard, and her head ached. She leaned back in the rocker and tried to relax . . . shoulders, arms, legs, toes. Maybe if she closed her eyes for just a couple of minutes, she would be able to see more clearly.

It was the last thought she remembered. When she opened her eyes again, silver-gray light filtered through the curtains, and a bird was trilling its wakeup call.

They hadn't come.

Disappointment swept away half-remembered

dreams. It was just after six; she tiptoed across the room and peered out into the hall. The bedroom doors were still closed. Jason would have given up and gone to bed hours ago, she thought. Today he would be tired and crabby or, worse yet, full of secret laughter at what he considered her foolishness.

It was no use trying to go back to sleep. Still dressed in yesterday's pants and T-shirt, she padded barefoot down the stairs, carrying her sneakers. This might be her last chance to sit out on the back porch and watch the first sunlight stream through the woods. Frank would probably call Greg and the Social Service people when he got to work and tell them he wanted Gwen to leave as soon as possible. Perhaps someone would come to take her away this very afternoon. . . .

She stopped at the kitchen door and stared in astonishment. Jason was sitting at the table, his head pillowed on his arms. An empty glass stood in front of him, and cookie crumbs littered the table.

"Jason, wake up." She held her breath, dreading what he would say when he realized he'd sat there all night for nothing.

"Jason?" He still didn't move. She touched his shoulder lightly and stepped back.

"What's the matter?" He sat up and looked

around groggily. "What — oh. Hi." He stretched and stood up. "Phew, I'm stiff!"

He didn't look angry or sound angry, not yet. Gwen watched anxiously as he wandered over to the window and stared out.

"I'm sorry — " she began, then realized he'd said the words at the same moment she said them.

"What are *you* sorry about?" she asked. "I thought you'd be mad at me."

Jason didn't look at her. "I'm sorry I gave you a hard time. About the ghosts. I really thought you were making it all up."

Gwen held her breath. "Don't you think so now?" she asked cautiously.

He shook his head. "I saw those guys you told me about. Right there." He pointed at the porch steps. "I heard them talking, too. When I switched on the light they disappeared, but for a few seconds" — now he turned to Gwen with a somber expression — "for a few seconds they were there, all right. Sure as we're standing here now."

They stared at each other. Jason shrugged and tried to force a smile, but it was no use. Gwen could tell he was as frightened as she was.

Chapter Seventeen

Even though she was certain Frank was calling Greg this morning, even though Dena drifted around the house all day looking pale and depressed, Gwen felt as if a weight had been lifted from her shoulders. Whatever happened next, there was one Mercy who knew she was telling the truth. Jason had seen the two men in the backyard. They had been carrying something; he agreed that it could have been a body. And he had heard their voices.

"It still feels like a bad dream," he said in answer to Gwen's excited questions. "I turned on the light because I thought there were real people out there, and I wanted to scare 'em off. And when I did, they just disappeared" — he snapped his fingers — "like that. There was no place for them to hide, but they were gone." He cocked his head at her. "What happened to you — fall asleep?"

Gwen nodded sheepishly. "I closed my eyes for a minute. . . ." She thought of something else. "Did you see anyone on the back stairs?"

"I fell asleep, too," Jason admitted. "It was the voices outside that woke me up. Tonight I'm going to stand by the window all night if I have to. I won't fall asleep standing up."

So he was ready, even eager, to watch again. "I'll stay awake, too," Gwen promised. "If I'm still here, that is. Are you going to tell your folks what you saw?"

"Nope." He didn't explain, but she was relieved. If he told Frank and Dena, they might think Gwen was trying to make more trouble by involving Jason. They might even assume he was lying to stop them from sending Gwen away. Better to stand watch again, she thought. Better to get proof.

But what kind of proof could it be?

"Letter for you, Gwen," Dena came out on the porch and dropped a long envelope on Gwen's lap. "Your brother — that's nice." She smiled wanly and stood next to the swing for a moment as if she wanted to say something else, then wandered back into the house.

Gwen picked up the envelope listlessly. A couple of weeks ago she would have torn it open, eager to read what Greg had to say, but now she was in no hurry. She could guess.

. . . I don't know where you got hold of this ghost nonsense, but I hope you can manage to forget it. Fast! I don't blame the Mercys if they're disgusted with you. . . . She folded the letter and stuffed it into the pocket of her jeans. Maybe she'd read the rest sometime, but not now.

That afternoon she went for a walk with Jason and Tessie. They waded through the tall grass in the meadow, explored the fringes of the woods, and walked through the sunflower field. They even sat on the bank of the river for a while and threw pebbles into the water, though Gwen was grateful when Tessie decided it was time to go home. The river made her uneasy; at any moment the sleepy little stream might change into a boiling torrent.

"You can come back for a picnic," Tessie said suddenly. "Lots of them."

It was the closest any of them had come to mentioning Gwen's departure, though it had been on Gwen's mind every minute. She had never loved the countryside more, had never felt more at home there. Why had it been so important to go to Phoenix? she wondered, as they started back between the rows of sunflower plants. Now, when she was no longer wanted at Mercy Manor, it seemed impossible that she had longed to leave.

There were stuffed pork chops, Gwen's favorite, for dinner that night. She watched Frank anxiously, but he said nothing about her moving, and she supposed he'd been unable to reach Greg. After dinner Jason helped to clear the table and then vanished upstairs. Dena and Gwen cleaned up the kitchen together, talking uncomfortably around long silences. Dena seemed more tense than ever. Gwen wished she could think of something comforting to say, but the thought of what she and Jason intended to do tonight kept her quiet.

At eight o'clock Gwen offered to put Tessie to bed, then retreated to her own bedroom to read and wait. Down the hall, she could hear the *tap-tap* of Jason's typewriter. She wondered if his play was nearly finished and if she'd ever have a chance to read it. Probably not. With a pang she thought of all the things she'd miss when she moved: Tessie's amusing chatter, the long talks and the Monopoly games with Dena, Frank's appealing mix of gruffness and warmth.

Quiet settled over the house. She put aside her book — she hardly knew what she'd been reading — and moved the rocking chair to the window. A three-quarter moon hung over the trees, and the stars seemed close enough to touch. I'll miss that, too, she thought. Until I moved out here I never knew how bright the stars could be.

She leaned back in the rocker and forced herself to take long, even breaths, trying to break the tension that stiffened her shoulders and turned her hands to ice. But the tension was not only inside her; it seemed to fill the house itself. She raised her arm to the windowsill and squinted at the time.

Midnight came and went — twelve-fifteen, twelve-thirty. The barest whisper of a step sounded in the hallway. Gwen tiptoed across the room and gripped the doorknob in both hands. Jason was waiting downstairs, she reminded herself; this time she wasn't alone.

She opened the door. The ghost-girl was waiting, not on the stairs this time but just outside the door, so close that the column of light filled the opening. Gwen leaped back and stared into the thin, sad face. There was pleading in the wide-set eyes, and a look of desperation.

She knows I'm going away. She knows this is the last chance she'll have to show me — whatever it is.

For what seemed a very long time, the girls faced each other, and then the column of light drifted toward the stairway. The ghost-girl looked back once, and then again. Satisfied that Gwen was going to follow, she glided down the stairs.

When Gwen reached the back hall, she saw Jason's tall figure outlined against the kitchen window, a lean shadow in the moonlight. The floor creaked, and he turned in time to see the ghost-girl move toward the half-opened basement door. Gwen heard his quick intake of breath, saw his involuntary jerk backward. She put a finger to her lips and waited. You have to come, she told him silently and felt a wave of relief and gratitude when he finally moved toward her.

By the time he had tiptoed to the top of the basement stairs, the ghost-girl had reached the bottom. She didn't look back again but seemed wholly intent on what was going to happen next. Gwen crouched on the second step and pulled Jason down beside her. She motioned toward the thin strip of light glowing beneath the fruit cellar door. Now he could see for himself that she had been telling the truth when she said someone had been in the fruit cellar the night Frank had confronted her in the basement.

The ghost-girl moved close to the door. Abruptly, it flew open in a burst of yellow light. Two figures filled the tiny room; behind them

Gwen saw the worktable cluttered with papers and boxes. For a moment the men glared at the ghost-girl, and then one of them reached out and dragged her into the fruit cellar. The door closed behind them with a muffled thud.

Gwen grabbed Jason's arm. "They're going to — " she began, but before she could finish the sentence, the door swung open again. This time the room was dark, but the two figures were easily visible, bathed in the silvery light that had surrounded the ghost-girl. One of them, the younger one, was carrying the girl in his arms.

"Move!" Jason's whisper seemed to come from miles away. "Gwen, get up!" She was being pulled backward, up one step and then another. At the top of the stairs, Jason drew her sideways, and they huddled in a corner of the hallway, not breathing as the men trudged past them and into the kitchen.

"This must be where they go outside." Jason slid along the wall and peered into the kitchen, then reached back for Gwen's hand. "They're gone."

Even before they had crossed to the window, Gwen heard the murmur of voices through the screen. She knew what they would see when they looked out. The men were at the foot of the porch steps. The younger one carried the girl, her long hair streaming. The older man held what looked like a heavy stick in his hand. They started across the lawn, exactly as Gwen had seen them before, and, as before, when the young man shifted his burden, a slim arm swung over his shoulder.

"They're going into the woods," Jason whispered. "Come on! We can't stop now."

She knew he was right. This was what she'd wanted, and now she had a witness to help her uncover the truth. But the thought of actually following the men into the woods was terrifying.

"Hurry up or we'll lose them!" Reluctantly Gwen followed Jason out to the porch and down the steps. "Faster!" They began to run toward the spot where the men had vanished among the trees.

"We won't be able to see!" Gwen gasped. "We can't — " She stopped protesting as they plunged into the woods and she saw the figures ahead of them glowing faintly in the dark.

"Keep moving," Jason ordered. "And for pete's sake, don't stumble. If we lose sight of them for even a minute, we're in big trouble. We might run into them head-on!"

Gwen shuddered. "I'm not going to fall on purpose," she panted. "I hate this!"

"I'm not exactly enjoying it myself." Jason gripped her hand more firmly. "But we've got to find out where they're going."

They hurried on, clinging to each other, until suddenly Jason stiffened his arm and held Gwen back.

"They've stopped," he muttered. "There's an open space up ahead."

They crept forward, ducking from one tree trunk to another. At the edge of a little clearing, they stopped to stare, spellbound, at the scene before them. The younger man had crouched and laid the girl on the ground. His companion lifted the stick he'd been carrying, and Gwen saw that it was a shovel. He began to dig, forcing the blade deep into the earth and tossing the dirt to one side. Up and down the ghostly tool swung, the blade thunking faintly as it bit into the soil.

"Let's go back," Gwen breathed. "Please, Jason! We know what they're doing. I don't want to watch!"

She looked up and saw that Jason was looking back the way they had come. Someone else was moving toward them, a frail, silvery wraith with short hair and wide, staring eyes. They clung to each other as the figure, its face a mask of horror, glided past them into the clearing. The digger stopped his work, and both men watched as she dropped to her knees beside the girl and began to cry.

The anguished sobs were too much for Gwen. "Come on!" she gasped, not bothering to whisper. "Jason!" She turned to run and screamed as a low-hanging branch swept across her cheek. When she looked back, the man who had been digging was coming toward them, the shovel raised over his head.

When Gwen recalled those next moments, it seemed to her that she and Jason didn't just run — they flew. Jason held her hand tightly and hurtled small gullies and logs, carrying her with him. The treacherous roots and fallen branches that had slowed their approach to the clearing were ignored; nothing mattered but that ghostly figure gliding toward them with the shovel raised like a club.

"We must be lost," Gwen gasped, when it seemed as if they had been running for miles. "We're going in the wrong direction!"

Jason didn't answer. With a last burst of effort, they broke out from under the trees, and Gwen felt a carpet of grass beneath her feet. Mercy Manor loomed ahead of them. Darkly forbidding in the moonlight, it had never seemed more beautiful to her. She risked a glance over her shoulder and saw there was no one — nothing — behind them.

At the foot of the porch steps Jason ended their headlong gallop.

"Whew!" He released Gwen's hand and turned toward the woods. "Is he coming?" He scanned the trees anxiously. "Man, I was never so scared in my life! When a guy comes after you with a shovel — even if he's a ghost — heck, *especially* if he's a ghost — " He drew a shuddering breath. "Guess we outran him — are you okay?"

"I think so." Gwen leaned against the railing. "Jason, what are we going to do? Those people are still out there, doing something terrible they must have done for the first time years ago. Why?"

Jason kept his eyes on the trees. "Maybe they have to," he said softly. "Maybe, like you said, they have to keep on doing it over and over until someone sees them and the truth comes out. Who knows!"

"Someone like us?"

"Right." He started up the steps backwards, as if he didn't dare turn his back on the dark woods. "So the first thing we have to do is make my folks believe what happened. And that won't be easy!"

"You mean you're going to wake them up and tell them *now*?" Gwen could picture the expression on Frank's face.

Jason led the way into the back hall. "In the morning," he whispered. "We'll tell them in the morning." But now he, too, sounded unsure. Gwen knew he was remembering how his parents had reacted to her stories of ghosts in the night. "They just have to believe us, that's all."

"We will," said a husky voice behind them. "Tell me what you saw."

Gwen gave a little shriek and whirled toward the kitchen door. Someone was sitting at the table.

Jason reached for the light switch and flooded the kitchen with light. Dena, huddled in her white robe, her face more strained than ever, looked at them tiredly.

"Tell me what you saw," she repeated. "I've been waiting. I have to know. Did they bury her in the woods?"

Chapter Eighteen

"You mean you knew all the time?" Gwen sank into a chair opposite Dena, and Jason levered himself onto the end of the counter. He stared at his mother incredulously.

"I didn't *know*," Dena said. "I didn't *know* anything. But — oh, dear." She broke off as heavy footsteps sounded overhead. "Now Frank's awake. He'll be furious. . . ."

They waited, like guilty children, till Frank thudded down the stairs and loomed in the doorway. His bright red bathrobe made him look a little like Santa Claus, but there was nothing jolly about his expression.

"What's going on here?" He glared at Gwen. "Are you seeing things again? I told you — "

Jason slid off the counter. "Dad, she was right

about the ghosts. Honest! It's all true!"

Frank's face flushed almost as red as his bathrobe. "Not you, too!" he exclaimed. "I might have known you'd be next. And I suppose you've gotten your mother into a state again. You ought to be ashamed!"

"I'm not in a state." Dena's voice was unexpectedly strong. "And Gwen and Jason aren't the only ones who are seeing things. I'm seeing what I should have seen years ago." She looked down at her hands clasped neatly on the tabletop. The knuckles shone white. "Ever since we moved here, I've been uneasy — you know that's true, Frank. At first it wasn't so bad, but the longer we lived here, the more sure I was."

"What do you mean?" Gwen asked breathlessly. "Sure about what?"

"That there was something important I should be remembering. Something that happened the summer when I lived here with Aunt Josie and Uncle Raymond and Allen — and Rose."

"Rose?" Gwen leaned forward, fearful that Dena would suddenly stop talking, as she had so many times before.

"Rose Michaelson. She was just about your age, Gwen, and she was a foster child, too. I guess Aunt Josie wanted a companion because Uncle Raymond was away so much — and when he was home, he spent more time with Allen than with her. At least, that was my impression. Rose and I became good friends that summer, even though I was only five. We were like you and Tessie, Gwen — together all the time — until the night she disappeared."

"Now wait a minute," Frank exploded, but Dena waved away the interruption.

"One day she was there, and the next she was gone. Policemen came to the house, and a social worker — that must have been the salesperson we met at the carpet store, Gwen. They all said Rose had run away from her last home and now she'd done it again."

"Nothing unusual about that," Frank snapped. "Kids never know when they're well-off." He glared at Gwen and Jason. "I don't see why we're talking about a runaway who took off thirty-some years ago — "

"Please!" Color was coming back into Dena's face. "I want to tell you about this. It's important, because I don't think Rose did run away. After all these years of assuming she's alive somewhere, I'm finally facing up to the truth."

Frank sighed heavily. Then he spread his big hands in a gesture of defeat. "Why have you changed your mind now?"

"I haven't changed my mind. I've *remembered*,

Frank, don't you see? I couldn't sleep tonight — I wanted to talk to Gwen, tell her how terribly sorry I was about how things turned out. Finally I went to her room, and she wasn't there. I looked out the window, just in time to see her and Jason going into the woods. I was going to call out to them, but suddenly I knew without a doubt they were following someone. And I remembered — all of it. What I'd seen the summer I was five and had made myself forget. It all came back."

"What came back?" Frank sounded as if he didn't want to hear the answer.

"The summer I stayed here, I had the bedroom Gwen has now, and Rose had Tessie's room. One night I heard her tiptoe downstairs, and a little later I saw Uncle Raymond and Allen go into the woods carrying something. I remember standing there at the window, too frightened to move. And after a while I saw Aunt Josie follow them. She must have been watching, too." Dena looked at Gwen. "That *is* what happened, isn't it?"

Gwen nodded. "We followed them into the woods, and we saw them digging a grave in a little clearing. It was awful!"

"But why would they kill her?" Jason wondered. "She was just a kid."

"Uncle Raymond was involved with a group of art thieves," Dena explained. "He died in prison when I was twelve or thirteen — I never told you that. And Allen worked with him. At the trial they said Uncle Raymond received stolen goods — paintings, jewelry, things like that. He kept the loot here for months, until it was safe to try selling it. The house was so isolated — more so then than it is now — and they didn't even have to use the roads. The stream was a real river then, before the dam was built. Uncle Raymond would arrange a meeting place miles from here and pick up and deliver things by boat."

"And Rose found out what they were doing?" Gwen asked. "Is that what happened?"

Dena nodded. "She must have. She and I used to play hide-and-seek all over this house, but we could never get into the fruit cellar because it was padlocked. Uncle Raymond and Allen spent a lot of time in there, and Rose told me she was going to find out what they were doing. I think that must have been when she started spying on them."

"So she followed them to the basement one night," Gwen said, "and they caught her and killed her."

"I doubt that they did it on purpose," Dena said quickly. "But Allen was sullen and short-tempered — he probably hit her in anger." She buried her face in her hands for a moment. "After that night, nothing was ever the same again. The next day Rose was gone, and Aunt Josie was sick in bed, and Raymond and Allen walked around looking like thunderclouds. I was mixed up and scared — a baby, really — with no one to talk to. I wanted to believe the people who said Rose must have run away. I *did* believe it. All these years I've remembered what fun I had that summer and made myself forget the rest. Till now."

"What happened to Allen?" Jason wanted to know.

"He went to prison, too, but just for a year or two. When he got out he went to California, and he was killed in a car accident. That was the final blow for Aunt Josie. She'd spent a lot of time in mental hospitals, and she finally died in one. My mother said it was shame over Raymond and Allen's imprisonment that killed her, but now I realize it was more than that. She knew what had happened to Rose, and she didn't tell. Think how guilty she must have felt!"

"And all this time, when you've talked about it being a mistake to move here — " Frank looked doubtful, but he was no longer arguing.

"Those were the times when I *knew* something was wrong and didn't know *what*," Dena explained. "I think Rose has been here in this house ever since we moved back. I even imagined I saw her a couple of times, and that made me sure I was going crazy. Poor thing, she wanted someone to know the truth about what had happened, and I wouldn't listen — not even when Tessie began seeing her, too. Then Gwen came, and Rose must have thought she had another chance to make someone believe. She must have seen you as a friend, Gwen — a person who would let the world know she wasn't just an ungrateful teenager who ran away from the people who had offered her a home."

Gwen shivered and leaned back in her chair. If Rose had seen her as a friend, then Raymond and Allen must have considered her an enemy. She remembered the day the grandfather clock fell and almost crushed her. Raymond and Allen could have made that happen, and Rose — she recalled that flash of gold in the dark basement — Rose had saved her.

"So what are we supposed to do now?" Frank demanded. "Turn the house over to a bunch of ghosts and move out?"

He was looking at Dena, but it was Jason who replied. "We can tell the police, Dad. Let them dig up the grave."

Frank groaned. "You're going to tell the police you saw ghosts and they led you to a grave in the woods? Come on! They'd laugh their heads off."

"We wouldn't have to do that," Dena said quickly, and Gwen realized she must have been doing a lot of thinking as she waited in the darkened kitchen for them to return to the house. "I'll tell them the truth — that I suddenly remembered what I saw that night, and I want them to look for a grave. Particularly in that little clearing. They'll do it, I'm sure."

"Maybe." Frank sounded doubtful but looked as if he'd run out of arguments.

"They will," Dena said confidently. "And then poor Rose can rest. Oh, Gwen, if it hadn't been for you, I'd never have faced up to this dreadful business. It's such a relief to have it out in the open."

"Jason was the one who said we had to follow the ghosts into the woods," Gwen said. "I wouldn't have done it alone — never, never, never! He's the one who said we had to find out what was going on. He wouldn't stop!"

"Well, that took nerve," Frank admitted, looking at Jason consideringly. "I've never seen a ghost and I don't intend to — but I doubt I'd follow one if the occasion came up." Jason's face glowed under his father's thoughtful gaze.

A door opened upstairs, and they heard Tessie call, then pad downstairs toward the light. She appeared in the doorway rubbing her eyes and yawning.

"What's the matter? Is Gwen going away now?"

There was a moment of silence, and then Frank cleared his throat. "No, she's not," he said gruffly. "What gave you that idea?" He held out his arms and Tessie climbed into his lap.

"You said she was. And I told you I didn't want her to go."

"I've said a lot of things." Frank grinned at Gwen, and then at Jason. Gwen knew it was the closest he could come to an apology. "Gwen's staying — if she wants to."

"I want to." Gwen struggled to find words to tell the Mercys how much she wanted to, but she felt tongue-tied. She hoped they could guess.

Dena pushed back her chair and stood up. "We'd better get some sleep," she said. "Gwen has a big day ahead in town with her friend." She came around the table and gave Gwen a hug. "You tell Julie to come out here next weekend," she suggested. "You can show her all around and have a picnic if you want. And she can meet your family."

About the Author

BETTY REN WRIGHT is the author of numerous books for young readers, including *A Ghost in the House*; *The Ghost Comes Calling*; two IRA-CBC Children's Choices, *Christina's Ghost* and *Ghosts Beneath Our Feet*; and *The Dollhouse Murders*, a nominee for the Mystery Writers of America's Edgar Allan Poe Award.

Ms. Wright lives in Wisconsin with her husband, George Frederiksen, who is an artist.

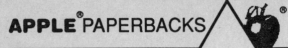